LOTUS BLOOM

AND THE

AFRO REVOLUTION

LOTUS BLOOM

AND THE

AFRO REVOLUTION

Sherri Winston

BLOOMSBURY
CHILDREN'S BOOKS
NEW YORK LONDON OXFORD NEW DELHI SYDNEY

BLOOMSBURY CHILDREN'S BOOKS
Bloomsbury Publishing Inc., part of Bloomsbury Publishing Plc
1385 Broadway, New York, NY 10018

BLOOMSBURY, BLOOMSBURY CHILDREN'S BOOKS, and the Diana logo
are trademarks of Bloomsbury Publishing Plc

First published in the United States of America in September 2022
by Bloomsbury Children's Books

Bloomsbury books may be purchased for business or promotional use. For information on
bulk purchases please contact Macmillan Corporate and Premium Sales Department at
specialmarkets@macmillan.com

Library of Congress Cataloging-in-Publication Data
Names: Winston, Sherri, author.
Title: Lotus Bloom and the Afro revolution / by Sherri Winston.
Description: New York : Bloomsbury Children's Books, 2022
Summary: Twelve-year-old Lotus Blossom, normally a peace-loving free spirit, must
summon the courage to fight against a racist dress code and stand up for herself.
Identifiers: LCCN 2021062837 (print) | LCCN 2021062838 (e-book)
ISBN 978-1-5476-0846-1 (hardcover) • ISBN 978-1-5476-0847-8 (e-book)
Subjects: CYAC: Middle schools—Fiction. | Schools—Fiction. | Student movements—Fiction.
| Friendship—Fiction. | African Americans—Fiction. | LCGFT: Fiction.
Classification: LCC PZ7.W7536 Lo 2022 (print) | LCC PZ7.W7536 (e-book) |
DDC [Fic]—dc23
LC record available at https://lccn.loc.gov/2021062837

Book design by John Candell
Typeset by Westchester Publishing Services
Printed and bound in the U.S.A.
2 4 6 8 10 9 7 5 3 1

To find out more about our authors and books visit www.bloomsbury.com
and sign up for our newsletters.

This book is dedicated to everyone who has ever faced a challenge and decided to stand up and do your thing! Right on, brothers and sisters. Right on!

LOTUS BLOOM

AND THE

AFRO REVOLUTION

When I look back, I can't help thinking that maybe I could have prepared for what was coming.

But of course, how could I?

Which led me to this moment. This place. Feeling the eyes of the whole town on me. Violin tucked against my chin. Bow hand trembling. A weird, terrifying pressure reaching way down in my spine. Fear and anger balled in a knot in the back of my throat.

All I ever wanted to do was play my music and be free to express myself. Yet, somehow, here I was.

What sparked the revolution?

Would you believe it all started with my bodacious afro?

And a paper airplane.

1

It's the first day of the new school year, and my breakfast Cheetos are exploding with flavor. A snare drum eight-count *RAT-A-TAT-tat*s on my tongue. I feel the joy of sunshine and the luxurious salty goodness of the cheesy powder covering my fingertips.

Me and my best friend, Rebel Mitchell, are walking to school together, as usual. Only this year she has to turn left after a few blocks, while I'll have one more block to go.

"I still can't believe you're ditching me!" she says.

So it is a regular morning in some ways; it's exactly the right time for Rebel's bad-mood morning scowl.

Filled with preteen angst and a revolutionary spirit, she is quite talented in the skill of scowl. She's got an impressive array, perfect for morning, noon, or night. She even has very special scowl-snarl combos for things like pep rallies, teen heartthrobs, and people who make hearts with their hands.

But when it comes to causes she believes in—and there are many—Rebel's intensity can be downright volcanic. What has her spewing lava this morning? The bright, shiny new performing arts middle school that opened near our neighborhood. Which happens to be the very building I'm heading to.

"I'm not ditching you!" I say. "We're going to different schools, that's all." I don't tell her that my heart is drumming double time and a symphony of self-doubt is running through my veins. I've been accepted into their music program. But am I good enough?

"Chill, Rebel," I continue. You know me, always trying to keep it light. "Have a Cheeto." I hold the bag toward her.

With each moist pop of a fingertip, the soft smack of my lips mimics soft piano in the key of A. (I am almost always thinking about music in some form or other.) I picture myself bowing the same note on my violin.

"I don't want your greasy, factory-polluted snacks," Rebel says, pushing the bag away.

Well! That was aggressive.

"And stop imagining musical notes while I'm talking to you, Lotus Bloom. What I want is for you to acknowledge how wrong this is."

"Rebel, can't you please be happy for me?" I grin, nudging her. I want—need—her to be happy for me. To lighten up. Be cool. *Chill.* But the eye roll she gives me is so cold I swear I see a penguin cross the road.

She stops, arms crossing over her chest, body weight resting into one leg. It's her listen-while-I-tell-you-about-yourself pose.

"Look, I know you think you can clear away 'bad vibes' by saying mantras or manifesting good stuff, and I usually like your throwback peace-and-love vibe like everything is 'groovy' or whatever, but this is important and it hurts that you don't seem to get it."

We're both silent for a moment, letting that sink in. A few cars whiz past. Miami Beach sparkles in the early morning, shades of aqua with streaks of pale golden sunlight.

I take a wet wipe out of my fanny pack and clean the Cheeto dust from my fingers. I want to show her she has my full attention.

Rebel draws a long breath. "When the stupid county had the opportunity to improve MacArthur Middle—*our school*—and the elementary school we went to in *our neighborhood*, what did they do instead? They chose to build that—that—"

She sputters sometimes when she's in full-rant mode.

"That tower of glass and steel and empty promises otherwise known as Atlantis School of the Arts." She ends with a loud huff and crosses arms. For emphasis.

We walk in silence for a few more paces. I glance at Rebel, wanting to take our annual back-to-school selfie. But with the smoke curling off the top of her head now, I think maybe I shouldn't.

"You know, Rebel, with your flair for drama, I told you to audition, too. You would have been accepted"—I snap my fingers—"just like that." I'm still trying to lighten the mood. Judging by her continued scowl, I can see I'm failing—hard.

"Everything is a joke to you, right?" she says. "You shouldn't be going to seventh at some fancy new magnet school. The money they used for that school should've gone to our school. And now they're stealing away talented kids like you! But that doesn't matter to you, Lotus, because you never take things seriously."

"That's not true, Rebel," I say softly. "I just don't like to take everything *too* seriously. And you know the funding isn't that simple." Not to mention, MacArthur kids weren't always, um, accepting of my throwback style!

I reach out and pull her into a hug, the way I've been doing since we were third graders and she staged a civil rights–style sit-in to protest greasy food in our grade school cafeteria. (Spoiler alert—she kicked their butts, and we got fresh fruit, and hamburgers once a week that came from quality cows.)

"Stop hugging me," she grumbles, but she is smiling. I feel it on her skin, the whisper of movement, me squishing her into my collarbone. She tries to push away, but I'm strong for a peace-and-love kinda chick. "Let go of me! Your stupid violin case is digging into my side. And you're smothering me with your *abundant* afro!"

I release her, and we both playfully push each other.

Two things I've always been known for—music and my 'fro. I've been rocking the woolly mammoth—Rebel's name for it—since forever. It takes me an hour to twist it up at night. But you can't be going to bed with your 'fro flying all over the head. 'Fro management is life. And when I take it down in the morning—POW! Afro explosion.

Our reflections move across the darkened windows of South Beach tanning salons, pawn shops, and Burger Kings as we continue up the street. I'm taller, darker, with eyes like my father's—dark and tilted at the corners. Rebel is shorter. Her face is rounder. Her light brown hair looks red in the morning light.

She's wearing a black tee, black jeans, black Chucks. I've got an ankle-length, apple-green granny skirt with tiny yellow flowers, a pink short-sleeved button-down, and light green sweater. My afro is a soft halo of fluff around my head, and it falls past my shoulders, held away from my face with a huge flower barrette. Her hair these days is shorter, split down the middle, and worn in puff balls over her ears.

How we look, our differences, never mattered to us. But more and more I am feeling the way they are yanking us in different directions. She is still my sister. Forever and ever. I just wish she would learn to relax.

"Life isn't one big chill party," she is saying. She has the amazing knack for reading my mind. Spooky. "MacArthur Middle is literally falling apart. Literally. Last year plaster fell off the ceiling into my hair. It's not fair!"

I nod. I remember that. We were in the media center, and a chunk of ceiling tile plopped right down on her head.

I am used to Rebel being intense. Her parents are both teachers, one at MacArthur—can you tell? But I won't let her ruin my big morning. I move toward my case.

"Don't you dare, Lotus!" She is shaking her head, but she knows she wants it. She needs it. She's gotta have it.

I take out my violin, my bow, leaving the case open on the sidewalk.

"I'll walk away!" she threatens. She won't. I know she won't.

My smile stretches all the way to my toes. I feel the rhythm of the road. The sounds of morning. Alicia Keys's "Girl on Fire" dancing off my strings and into the air. Long time ago, Rebel adopted the girl power anthem as her theme song.

"Stop it!" she demands, but I keep playing. I feel the power of the song, the intricacies of the finger work along the slender neck of my instrument. I feel my soul lift into the clouds.

Finally, I exhale, and the energy, the joy I put into the song still lingers.

We start laughing, a little at first, then a lot. I knew it would work.

"That was amazing!" says a passerby. She's with two other ladies, all of them dressed in workout clothes and carrying brightly colored gym bags in a palette of primary colors. "You're as good as a professional!"

"Believe me, she knows!" Rebel says. I snap my case shut

after replacing my violin and bow, and my best friend yanks me farther down the sidewalk.

We are laughing now like we used to.

I've always been good at getting Rebel to laugh.

But can it last?

She glances up the street. We are almost to Sixty-Fourth Ave. When we reach the corner, I cross Alton and go toward the ocean. First time since third grade that we are going in different directions.

It's not only scary, it hurts. I know she's nervous, too.

We walk without talking, letting the music of the traffic and the wind in the trees wash over us and soothe our nerves. Then we reach the corner. Rebel chews her lip, and I bounce my eyebrows up and down. We fist-bump lightly.

"Later, girl," she says.

"Hey," I say. "No fights on the first day, hear?"

She snorts a laugh. "I ain't promising nuttin'," she says in her best tough-girl accent. We both ignore the tiny tear glistening in the corner of her eye.

Traffic clears, the light changes, and I cross, away from MacArthur, away from all the friends I'd grown up with. And Rebel.

I turn my back and keep moving forward.

2

After me and Rebel go our separate ways, I brace myself for my first day. I'd heard about the cutthroat atmosphere at some performing arts schools. I mean, I've watched the reboot of *Fame* and seen every *Step Up* movie ever made.

But it turns out, at this school, a lot of kids just mind their own business. At first, at least.

Atlantis is a spanking brand-new performing arts school for grades seven to nine. It was supposed to open a while back, but, you know, everybody got the plague, so . . .

Soon as I found out two years ago they were building it near my neighborhood, I prayed I'd be good enough to get in. Dad still lived here in Miami back then. We'd walk over to the work site to check out the progress.

School starts today, Monday, but for some reason seventh grade doesn't have anywhere to go until Friday. I think the administration forgot we were coming.

We are going to spend the whole week—all 129 seventh graders—hanging out in the school's PAC (performing arts center), mainly with Mrs. Nan, a music teacher for our grade.

One boy, Nico something, plays with the lighting so we can snap our selfies and not look like a bunch of shadows.

#woollymammoth #AtlantisSchool #TomorrowsStars

I'm antsy about the delay, wanting to just start already. But the truth is, if we'd gone straight to class, I might not have met Dion. His first words to me: "Girl! You are my new muse!"

He likes my throwback style—especially my 'fro. I like how confident and loud and proud he is. He looks—is—beautiful. You didn't see boys in eyeliner and lip gloss at MacArthur. Seventh grade is going to be REALLY different. I can tell.

Dion is in visual arts. He starts sketching me, like, on the spot. He's really good, getting the look just right as he sings, "Girl, that hair is *beeeeyonnnnnd!*"

#MuseForADay

Performing arts schools definitely attract a certain type. I tell Dion that he reminds me of the jazzy, snazzy New Orleans blues song "When the Saints Go Marching In." He says that song is as gay as he is, so why not!

It's nice to have a friend. Meeting him helps ease the pain of being apart from Rebel. As the days go on and I don't see her on my walks to school the rest of the week, I'm thinking she is ghosting me, or at least still mad? Since I saw her, I've sent her lots of silly and encouraging texts; she sent back excuses and one-word responses. I try not to think too much of it.

☙

Friday, I am dressed for success and ready to do my thing. *Finally*, they pass out our schedules.

CLASS	TIME
Music Block	7:50–9:30
Piano Adv	7:50–8:40 (rm 111)
Orchestra Beg	8:45–9:30 (rm 200)
Math/Science Block	9:40–noon
Lunch	noon–12:45
Lang Arts/Civics Block	12:50–2:30
French	2:30–3:30

Dion half closes his eyes and launches into a dramatic goodbye:

"My dear, '*You know the place between sleep and awake? That place where you still remember dreaming? That's where I'll always love you*' . . . Peter Pan. I'll be waiting, muse."

I can't help it; I burst out laughing. It feels good to release some of the pent-up tension.

He does a cutesy finger wave, then struts toward the visual arts building, never to be seen again—until lunch, anyway. I head to the piano lab.

Piano lab.

It's enough to make me swoon. At my old school we were lucky to have a dingy room that smelled like pee and Pine-Sol with a piano in it and walls that didn't have mold. And when we were out of school because of the whole pandemic disaster, music period was eliminated. None of us could even imagine anything like this.

A Piano *lab.*

Individual keyboards with headphones.

Plug in and only you can hear your music.

Most of my practice and music study so far has come from private tutors. It's not that we're rich—pursuing passion *ain't* cheap!—but I'm lucky. My dad made music education a priority.

Here, our piano teacher, Mr. Teegan, can put on his headphones and talk to us through the computer or listen to us play. So *dope*!

He explains how the class will work and how he grades, but I find it hard to listen because I can't stop playing with the keyboard and trying to write songs and thinking about how truly truly truly TRULY happy I am.

A girl named Mercedes sits beside me and tosses her long brown hair. She's feeling my retro look and tells me my sense of style is "beyond."

She herself looks modern and sleek in white jeans (tight) and a hot pink top (also tight). When I saw her earlier in the PAC, it was clear she was really pretty and she was used to getting attention. But she seems nice. We whisper back and forth in class, which is really fun. Meeting her takes away some more of my anxiety. Dion and his Gay All-stars— their name for themselves—are great, but I was hoping for some girls to hang with, too.

Cool as Mercedes is, though, I feel a hole open up inside me. An actual ache in my chest. It's only been a week, but I miss Rebel.

I take in deep breaths to center myself. *Woo-saaah!*

🪷

In my next period, I know I'm actually going to need a bucket of chants and woo-saaahs.

Mrs. Nan, the seventh-grade orchestra director, asks us to officially introduce ourselves by playing a little of one of our favorite pieces. (What a wonderful world it would be if everyone had to introduce themselves with a song. Just saying!)

Anyway, mine is a violin solo, Vivaldi op. 3. Upbeat, cheery, with a lot of spirit—like me!

When I finish, Mrs. Nan has a shocked expression on her face. "Did you play that at your audition?"

"I . . . didn't have to audition."

I say it very humbly so I won't come off like I'm stuck up. I will never forget the day I got my invitation letter in the mail. That *thang* is still tacked to the wall in my bedroom. I even wrapped fairy lights around it. Mom kept telling me to "slow my roll" (which makes me laugh because anytime Mom tries to use slang it sounds hilarious). But Dad was so proud. He said I was good enough and I should take advantage of every opportunity because regular public schools didn't really do a lot for kids in the arts.

Our video call lasted a whole hour that day. I miss him so much.

Mrs. Nan looks up from the computer, and something in her expression makes my breath catch.

"I'm going to send an email. You need to be in the main orchestra room."

Um . . . *what*?

Eighth and ninth graders have classes in main orchestra. That makes my heart drum marching-band style.

I am freaking out.

I go into the main orchestra room half expecting a scene from one of the old Westerns Granny likes. You know, where a stranger walks into an old-timey saloon, and the whole place goes silent?

But I am merely an insignificant seventh grader, and nobody gives me a second look.

Well, someone does whisper, "Look at all that hair!"

I squeeze past oboes, cellos, winds, and other strings, to a desk where a tall man stands talking to two other kids.

Only it isn't just some tall dude with salt-and-pepper hair. Soon as he turns, I know. It is The Man. My heart *literally* stops in my chest.

(If my language arts teacher hears I said that, tell her I'm being as literal as I can be.)

Four feet in front of me is Maestro Santiago Vasquez.

L E G E N D.

I knew he helped set up Atlantis's music program. Even so, I did *not* know he was part of the faculty. I hadn't expected to meet him until I could audition for the county youth orchestra when I turn thirteen (in ten months, eleven days, but who's counting?).

But there he is.

Former Cuban refugee turned international violin virtuoso.

I give him the note from Mrs. Nan, unable to look at him. You don't look a L E G E N D in the eyes. YOU. DO. NOT.

Should I curtsy or ask for his autograph? So much is going through my head, it feels surreal.

He gives me a long look, like he's amused. Then he says, "So you're too advanced for beginners?" His tone makes it clear he doesn't quite believe this is true.

My heart thumps in my throat. Have I swallowed it? (Literally?)

Someone cracks about my throwback outfit—jeans, pegged above the ankle, with a totally '70s bohemian peasant blouse, white with yellow flowers. Whatever; secondhand clothes are life.

Someone else says, "Look at that hair!" again. This time several kids laugh.

Yes! Behold my glorious crown!

Even Maestro Vasquez smiles. So I exhale.

Woo-saaah! Woo-saaah!

He tells everyone, "Class, instruments down. I need everyone in their proper place. And silent, please."

His slight Spanish accent made his words sort of lilt at the ends like flower petals bending toward the light. I was sure he wanted everyone to sit because he wanted to see where to put me.

Nope!

"Let us hear you play?" Maestro Vasquez says.

My face, my feet, everything goes numb.

3

N-Now?" I stammer. I feel my eyeballs starting to sweat. This isn't the same as playing on the sidewalk, or for people my age. If I had to make a list of what would be my most stressful situations EVER, playing for Maestro Vasquez—unprepared—would be at the top!

He gives me his semiamused look again. I feel love and death and agony and joy all at once.

I am going to play for him. My idol.

I want to float through the air.

I want to sink through the floor.

I breathe in deep. My hair moves around me like a woolly guardian angel. A well-moisturized and swingy guardian angel!

But I am definitely sweating. I say a little prayer.

'Fro, don't fail me now.

All that is left is to play. So I do. Vivaldi op. 3. Same as I played for Mrs. Nan.

Soon as I start, I get that same feeling. Like I am drawing power and courage and grace with each note, each movement.

It is always the same. I get lost in the music. I can't see, think, feel anything but the notes and melodies turning into . . .

light

inside

of me.

The pace is fast, and I am back in the time of Vivaldi, on the streets of Amsterdam in 1711 when he wrote it, strolling through a watercolor world built of eighth notes and joy.

I breathe in the notes and push them out through the strings while keeping time with the rhythm. Foot rocking enough to sway my 'fro, and I feel my whole self smiling because the music is a heartbeat sending fire through my veins. I am pure light, shining for the whole world.

Whenever I finish a piece, I am flooded with warmth, then a twinge of sadness that it is over. I no longer see the beautiful colors or feel the notes or picture Amsterdam in the eighteenth century. I am back to the real world.

Maestro Vasquez is in the real world, too, and he no longer looks amused.

Is that good? Bad? Do I have Cheeto dust on my face? I have no clue.

Every serious musician has dreams of one day performing in a concert hall. I have that fantasy approximately 157 times a day. (Rough estimate.)

In my fantasy, hundreds of guests are sitting in the audience, wearing their evening gowns and cummerbunds and fancy jewels. All there to hear me—the virtuoso prodigy from Miami Beach, Florida, Lotus Leandra Bloom.

Doves—the kind that don't poop in your hair—fly over the audience dropping love and satisfaction.

And I will give the performance of my life! Lights fading. Curtain down. Mic dropped. Of course, in your fantasies, you're fearless.

When I return from that little trip to fantasy island, the maestro is staring quizzically at me.

I stammer again. Can't believe I am so nervous "Sh-sh-should I play something else?"

He pauses for a minute, then says, "Where did you learn to play baroque style so well?" And instead of answering I stand there, shrugging like an idiot. Sensing confusion, he says, "Baroque style? Do you know what that is?"

Of course I do! But my words keep tripping out of my mouth. "Um . . . Baroque means when you imagine that your bow is shorter and you have to make your strokes shorter . . ." but I stop when he gives me *that* look.

"Thank you, miss, *I* know what it means."

Woo-saaah, girl. Keep it together.

He gives me a really strange look, then stares off into space. I hear whispers. A weird sort of tension forms like a cloud over the whole orchestra room. Is he anti meditation?

Maestro asks if I am familiar with the Bach Double.

I tell him yeah.

He grabs a violin off his desk. I realize then that he plans to ask me to play—WITH HIM!!!

The entire class presses in around me, and something squeezes in my chest. I am so scared my eyeballs start sweating again.

He takes the lead, and his pace and tone are mellow and smooth. I don't have time to worry because it is my turn to play and I can't think about it too long or I'll miss my entrance into the piece, so I just play and he plays and we are playing *together* and it feels A M A Z I N G.

After we finish there is applause from the whole room. Electric fireflies zing through my blood. He asks me how long I've been playing.

"Since I was four or so," a voice says from somewhere deep inside me.

My neck muscles strum as tight as my violin strings. I just know that if he says anything negative or mocks me or tells me I am just a kid who should go back to the beginning, I'll die right there. Fall through the earth. Turn to stone.

But that's not what happens. He starts talking again, in this real soft voice:

"You are exceptionally gifted. Musicality is so hard to teach. You possess remarkable musicality for a musician of your age and experience. The ability to feel the music and make others feel it, too. I believe you would make an excellent concertmaster for our orchestra, as others here would benefit from watching someone of your caliber." Then he dips his head at me, sort of a bow.

I am speechless.

He turns toward the class. "Adolpho, you will please move to first chair, second section. The rest of second section, please move down one seat, accordingly." Maestro turns to me. "And Miss . . . your name, please?" I tell him again, and when he says, "Miss Lotus Bloom," my name sounds like candy in his mouth. "Miss Bloom will be first-chair violin in section one. Everyone, meet your new concertmaster."

More applause, but lighter, with an air of *Oh no he didn't!*

The Adolpho kid looks like he just swallowed his bow. His cheeks turn a violent shade of red. It's clear he thinks he had earned his seat.

He's not happy. "I am supposed to get first chair, section one. I'm a ninth grader. My mom said . . ."

Maestro is already shaking his head. "I'm sure your mother has been very encouraging; however, as you know, I have been evaluating all of you this week and . . . I had made no final choice for concertmaster. I simply let you assume the role until I could be sure. Now, I am sure."

Then he tells Adolpho to move. I feel bad for the kid and a little nauseous for myself.

"I think your technical skill would work well there," Maestro is saying in my direction. And before I know it, I am sitting in an orchestra seat prewarmed by Adolpho. I can literally feel a chorus of cymbals clattering in my soul.

Once the whispering and not-so-subtle looks calm down, Maestro gets down to business.

"Orchestra, I have some important dates that you must respect," he says, words dancing from his lips like poetry. "Muy importante! Saturday, November fifth. It is our first production. We will demonstrate to your parents, the community, and faculty why we built the Atlantis School of the Arts, and why ours is the best youth orchestra in the state."

Then he tells us we have two other smaller shows to get us comfortable playing together before the big show:

Sept. 23—a musical set at a Freedom High School game.

Oct. 4—open house.

For the rest of the morning, my head buzzes in high C. I am so tripped out from the experience I really don't hear, see, or smell much of anything. (I do crave more Cheetos, however.)

A few kids pause at my seat to congratulate me or say, "Nice job," but others throw me curious looks.

Ha ha. Nothing to see here. Just your average seventh-grade earth mama.

All through the week, I had been swapping stories with Dion about how much I hoped to become concertmaster one day. The first step toward my big future in music.

I had no idea it'd be happening so fast.

I'm happy to see that Taj, another dude I met during our week in the PAC, is also in the advanced orchestra. He says it's good to see another seventh grader, and I agree. Then he chucks me in the arm and heads to the instrument lockers before I can say anything further.

Did I mention that Taj's looks are *bangin'*? Dion has been crushing hard on him, but alas, he is convinced Taj only has eyes for "the ladies." (I think so, too!)

Taj is in the percussion section.

Boom-boom-boom!

Seeing him makes me swallow hard and think about things like whether or not he has a girlfriend or what he thinks about tall, thin girls with rich cocoa brown skin and giant afros who play the violin. But I shake my head—this is not the time; if this is going to be my path, I need to focus on music.

Distracted with everything going through my head, I turn in my seat. And that is when I feel a weird poke. A demi-poke. On my scalp. Which is weird because . . . almost nothing ever makes its way past the woolly mammoth.

I shake my head, and a paper airplane falls to the ground.

I pick it up, trying to figure out where it came from. I scan behind me. No one is looking at me, and most of the seats are empty.

Tatiana Lee, the second-chair violin, is next to me. An Asian American girl with her hair parted down the center and pulled in two bottlebrush ponytails, she is wearing a vest covered in patches with sayings like Hippie; Don't Tread on Me; It's Bad Luck to Be Superstitious; and Peace. Maybe we'll get along.

23

"Looks like you've made an admirer," she remarks. But she's not smiling.

"I'm going to give you a quick lesson about Adolpho Cortez. I'm an eighth grader, but I've known him since I was a little kid. We live in the same neighborhood. His parents, the Doctors Cortez, are power obsessed. They see themselves as Titans. Big shots who helped make this school possible. 'Dolpho seems to think he's Prometheus, the Greek god who gave fire to humans, and he's determined to show his Titan daddy that he is a musical star."

Then she grabs her stuff, stands, and looks back at me with a crooked smile. "By the way, Maestro was right. Your musicality is dope, and your playing is *amazing*. But watch yourself. Adolpho can be vicious when he doesn't get his way. His parents are even worse! He's a tool, and I'm glad he got moved, but be warned. He has clout, and he doesn't like to lose!"

I call out before she leaves, "Do you resent that I got leapfrogged over you, too? I don't want anyone to be mad at me." The realization I may have more than one enemy is hitting me for the first time.

She blows out a sigh.

"Girlfriend, the music world can be brutal—even at our level. You can't make friends with everybody. You have to be true to yourself and your work. As for you getting picked over me, I'm not thrilled about it. But I'm more thrilled about it than sitting second chair to that robot Adolpho. Besides, one of these days, I may just bump you off your seat."

Then she turns and disappears through the back door.

I blink. *What* just happened?

Then I realize I am still holding the airplane that had crash landed in my hair. What do you do when some random guy hits you with a little piece of paper?

Is it worth obsessing over?

No, it isn't.

Someone threw a paper airplane.

Big deal.

But I might have other things to worry about.

4

First thing I do when I roll over in bed Saturday morning is grab my phone. Want to check for missed calls.

None.

I felt like the empty screen is screaming: *"HE'S BUSY!"*

It's almost one in the afternoon in Paris. What is there to do on a fall afternoon, anyway? Only about a million things, sigh. I drop my phone back onto the bed.

I try to picture my dad at one of those outdoor cafés, wearing a beret and sipping from a tiny European espresso cup. It makes me laugh out loud, then I immediately cover my mouth. No need to chance Mom coming in here to "check on me."

She is always "checking on me." What does that even mean? I'm a twelve-year-old middle school girl. Seventh grade. Orchestra. Performing arts student. Violin wizard. (Hey, it's not healthy to deny your god-given gifts. That's what Daddy likes to say.)

But Mom . . . not so much. She is not a fan.

And that is why I just know if I could get out to Paris with Dad, life would be so different.

It's still before seven in the morning, but I want to get out of the house as soon as possible. Weekends are not off-days for #woollymammoth, though. She has to be fluffed and patted and knick-knack-pattywhacked.

So the morning 'fro-a-thon begins:

First, I jump in the shower to get some moisture into my hair without totally drenching it. I use my fingers to undo the four sections I twisted up the night before.

Then I get out of the shower and rub my favorite leave-in conditioner into my hair. (Not too much. If your hair has too much moisture, the 'fro won't stand up.)

Finally, I stand before the mirror and alternate between picking and fluffing, fluffing and picking. My old-school afro pick with its metal teeth and black plastic handle shaped into an upraised fist—Rebel got it for me, if you couldn't guess—is perfect for bringing height to my hair.

When I'm done, I study myself in the mirror. Today's 'fro is truly a work of art, if I do say so myself. And I do, I do!

No matter what else happens in the world, I feel confident about that. I take pride in how I look.

But then Mom pops into my head and I wince involuntarily.

Mom is beautiful. Round face, large round eyes, and skin a pale brown. When I think about it, it's impossible to ignore

27

the obvious differences between us. My features are dark, angular. My skin a warm, deep shade of brown. My eyebrows are thick, almost caterpillar-like. I am all about style. My mom used to love dressing up. Now she's more interested in launching her business, whatever that happens to be. (It changes monthly.) Most of me looks about as distinct from her as possible. But I do look just like him.

Like Daddy.

I'm sure she doesn't love to remember that.

But I do have Mom's hair. Thick, long, beautiful hair.

Although, while I am the captain of #TeamAfro, Mom is a staunch believer in relaxers. #TeamBoneStraight. She can't function unless her 'do is shining and laid flat.

I am no snob, mind you. Live and let live.

But she doesn't understand my commitment to maintaining my afro, which feels like a huge part of my identity to me. If I don't hassle her for what she does to her hair, why should she be in my business about how I do mine?

Right on cue, as I am speed-eating my Frosted Flakes, here comes Mom and her boo, Derrick. The fact that he stays here with Mom makes me a little sick. She could do so much better.

"Up early on a Saturday morning," Derrick says. Yuck! I try to be kind to everybody, but what could you say to someone who can't help stating the obvious.

"Yup!" I say, my spoon rattling in my bowl as I finish my last scoop.

"Hey, baby," Mom says. "Where're you going so early?"

"The beach. I'm going to sit in that little park area and practice," I say. I leave out, "like always."

"I see you've fluffed up that 'fro. Girl, your life would be so much easier if you let somebody relax that hair," she says. See what I mean?

I grab my violin case, brush a kiss against her smooth, round cheek, and head for the door. "See you later, Mom. I have my phone if you need me."

See why I couldn't wait to get out of the house?

❧

The walk takes fifteen minutes. By the time I'm sitting on a bench, facing the ocean, it's almost nine. A breeze pushes the blanket of salty sea froth onto shore, and each time the ocean exhales it ruffles the sand. I need to clear my head, and this is my zen spot.

My violin rests against my face like it belongs there. I draw in a deep breath and blow it out through my nose. After repeating that process a few times, I begin.

The Sibelius piece always feels like a question. So urgent and delicate and necessary. The notes move over one another in a slow buildup of agony and longing. At a key moment in the concerto, I imagine the deep-throated bassoon's resounding interjection that comes when an orchestra plays the piece.

My eyes are shut to the world. I am no longer on the park

bench facing the ocean, listening to the applause of the waves. I am floating high above the world where best friends might be ignoring you and mothers definitely don't understand you.

A world where fathers don't pick up the phone or call you back when you need them.

I feel my body push off the bench, never stopping or pausing the song. The air around me moves in a rhythm, and my 'fro sways rhythmically in the breeze. All the hurt and frustration of the past week pours like liquid fire through my veins, flows into my fingertips and down my bow, and wafts out through the strings.

Rebel and me; me and Rebel, we'd always had each other's back. Being at Atlantis was an important part of my journey. I want her there—if not at the school then at least, you know, at my side spiritually.

My mini concerto gains intensity. My elbow dances as I raise, extend, and withdraw the bow at a furious pace. Behind my eyelids I see palm tree silhouettes vibrate against a rosy sky.

Ocean air, tangy and salty, fills my insides, sealing all the spaces where the music can't reach.

A sound, a noise, draws me back to earth, but my eyelids remain shut. Then the song leaves my body. It's over, and I feel its end like a small loss. Slowly, I let the ocean, the sand, and the sky back in.

Several people have gathered. Normally, first thing on a

Saturday morning, I don't draw a crowd—which is the point, for me, at least. But they are applauding, and when I say, "Thank you," only then do I feel the single tear on my cheek.

Rebel is standing to one side, holding her dog Maya's leash. One look and I can tell she wants to apologize, but as usual she doesn't know how.

I finish thanking the strangers, then turn to Rebel and say, "What's up?" I try to keep my tone light, but . . . admittedly, I am feeling a little salty. I've texted her several times, and she's been basically ghosting me all week.

Her dog is small, some kind of beagle, with caramel and white fur. "Hi, Maya. Hello, girl," I coo, and crouch down to pet her. She wags her tail, and her whole butt goes back and forth. I giggle.

"I was just out walking Maya," Rebel says.

Both me and Maya give her a look, like, "Girl, boo!" I stand. Rebel flops down on the bench, and I join her. We both know she is lying. This is my spot. Her usual walks with Maya go the opposite direction.

But I don't want to pick a fight.

"How was your first week of school?" I ask, kicking my feet back and forth. Something I always did when I was a little kid. When I felt awkward.

She shrugs. "It was all right." She glances at me with a look that says, *"How much longer are we going to have silly small talk?"*

I'll bite. "Okay, Rebel, what's really up? What brought you down here so early in the morning on the weekend?"

She sighs. "I felt kinda bad about Monday; how we left things, I mean."

"Me too."

We are silent for several minutes. It's late August. Still summer break for people from other states. Tourist families strolled along Ocean Drive behind us. In Florida, our schools start two or three weeks before Labor Day.

I glance at the path and see a Black woman and a little girl—her daughter?—coming toward us. She has short, natural hair and a wide face and grin.

"I just had to get closer and see that beautiful hair," the mom says. She gazes at my hair like it's a magic trick. This happens a lot with Black women. Especially other naturals—women who don't use harsh chemicals to straighten their hair.

"Thank you," I say.

"You are welcome. I just hope one day my 'fro is as audacious as yours. Well, you girls have a good morning!"

See? That is how you approach somebody about their hair. A lot of non-Black folks would come right up and try to touch it. Like I was some exotic creature in a petting zoo.

Rebel lets out a short bark of laughter.

"You and that hair!" she says. She tries to smile, but then her face closes up.

I reach down and scoop Maya onto my lap. I ask, "What's wrong?"

32

She shakes her head.

"Nothing, except school doesn't seem right without you," she says.

I take a gulp of air and try to ignore the headache forming behind my golden-lens shades. I am aware that she has not asked how *my* week had been, but I let it go. Sometimes Rebel's manners are on strike. Still, I push ahead.

"Tell me, Reb, what's happening? What's the talk? The scoop? The business? Did you get Mr. Birmingham for history?" I'm being extra smiley and upbeat. It's my default. The setting I turn on when I'm in doubt.

She spends the next five or ten minutes catching me up on what some of our old friends are doing.

And yes, she did get Mr. Birmingham, which is important because Rebel is absolutely in love with him, even though she claims it is all about his syllabus and not at all about his pretty brown skin and long eyelashes. *Yeah, girl, what*ever.

"Did they bring the music teacher back?" I ask gently. I know I'm heading into dangerous territory.

"No, they didn't," she says. Then she looks at me, pinning me with one of her darkly intense gazes. It's like being held in place by the strongest hand ever. I try to look away but can't.

Finally, I squawk, "What?" I feel heat flood my cheeks. Hear my heartbeat kick into half-note drumbeats.

She blows out a long sigh.

I recognize that sigh.

I've avoided that sigh.

It means trouble. It means I am about to have a fight with my best friend. It means I can already hear my heart splintering from the bluntness I know is coming. I brace myself.

"You should be there, with me. With us," she begins. Her wide-open expression has closed into a tight fist of frustration and even anger. "I still can't believe you ditched Mac-Arthur for that new school."

She flings her fingers in the general direction of Atlantis.

"But you said yourself they didn't bring the music teacher back, which means . . ."

"Nothing!" she says. She's becoming more and more animated now. "So MacArthur doesn't have a music program. So what? You've been taking private lessons since you were four, learning violin and piano from your dad since you were three. You play so well you could teach. Do you really need a fancy music department?"

Yes, I do.

I swallow hard. The wind kicks up and tugs at my 'fro. The air is growing warmer despite the breeze off the ocean. On the horizon, gray clouds are knitting together. Any South Floridian could tell you they promised rain in the day ahead.

"Rebel, you want to major in politics when you go to college. You don't play an instrument, you don't . . ."

Now her animation amps up even more.

"I don't need to play an instrument to know what I know.

And I know that there are more important things in life than music!"

"To you, maybe. But not me. Music is my life!" My tone practically begs for understanding. I don't get it.

"Don't be so dramatic, Lotus!"

My heart is pounding, and my temper is starting to rise. I take several cleansing deep breaths before speaking.

"You shouldn't be so dismissive, Rebel." I'd learned that word "dismissive" from a counselor at school last year. Mrs. Jones. She overheard one of my and Rebel's disagreements and saw how Rebel reacted to me not agreeing with her. *"She's being rather dismissive of your feelings, don't you think?"* she'd said. I did think.

"Maybe if you stayed, you could, you know, be the change the school needs. We could go to school board meetings. Protest. Get some support. You could help, be part of changing how the county treats MacArthur Middle and Bayside Elementary," she says.

Now she's standing, hands on her hips. Where I am taller and thinner, Rebel is softer and shorter. Her red 'fro is short, the typical puff balls today replaced by one poof pushed back from her face. She's looking down at me with her Sojourner Truth pose: Rebel on the Mount, speaking before a crowd of one. Well, two if you count Maya. I stand, cradling her fat little beagle like a baby. I soothingly pat the dog's back, but I don't feel soothed at all. I'm getting pretty ticked off.

"Um, Rebel, I love you like a play cousin, but you really

need to chill. I'm not your enemy. You have a problem with the school board, not with me."

"It's the same problem!" she practically shouts. If we're drawing attention now, it's not because of my bodacious 'fro. "Stop thinking about yourself for once, Lotus. There are bigger things going on, and if you weren't so eager to sell us out and go to the other side . . ."

It's my turn to cut her off.

"Did you just call me a sellout? I'm no sellout. I'm loyal to all my friends and my beliefs." Maya squeals, and I realize with the quickening of my pulse, I've begun to squeeze the poor doggie tighter and tighter. I sit her on the ground. Rebel picks up the leash.

"All I know is you leaving gives the county one more reason to think they're doing the right thing. And the fact that you want to act like it doesn't matter at all, well, it makes you look really ignorant and unfeeling!"

It's like being slapped. So I'm a sellout? Is that what she thinks of me?

Hot tears prick at the corners of my eyes. On the horizon, the dark clouds continue their march across the sky, moving steadily toward the shore. Today's afternoon showers will arrive before noon.

I'm still struggling to pull myself together when Rebel hits me with her parting shot:

"Why is it so hard for you to want to make a difference? What are you afraid of?"

She stomps off. Exit, stage right. Another dramatic production from the Rebel Is Always Right Theater.

I pick up my violin, determined to wash out my brain with music. But her assault left me winded and wounded. For one of the rare times in my life, music can't completely soothe me.

Not when a question keeps jabbing at my brain.

Could she be right?

5

Monday, I'm happy to wake up feeling sassy and classy.
I do some yoga, and it gets a little funky; old-school Motown
is just what I need.

I post new snaps on my social media. #funkyhotyoga
#RESPECT #Aretha #woollymammothfro. The woolly
mammoth is getting longer and stronger. I'm feeling all good
vibes and positivity.

The posts almost immediately get likes from Dion, then
Mercedes, then Tatiana, and then . . . *Rebel*.

Starting the day with likes—#Winning! But what's that
supposed to mean?

I ditch the bus to walk to school. Guess who does the same?

                    REBEL:

    "Hey! Wait up?"

                    ME:

    (keeps walking)

HER:

(shouting) "HERSHEY! YOU KNOW YOU HEAR ME!!"

ME:

(trying to not laugh) "No, I don't."

I try mean-mugging her, which works for about two seconds. My stink eye needs serious work.

Rebel has always been formidable, despite being the height and size of a Smurf. I have to look down to talk to her. She has pale yellow skin, a slight space between her top front teeth. She's been rocking puff balls since first or second grade. And she has curves.

When she throws her arm around my waist, I think, *Uh-oh*. What's up?

Rebel is all smiles. Rebel Mitchell is NEVER super smiley. Especially after Saturday.

I play it cool.

"You called me a 'sellout.'"

"I'm really sorry about that," she says. "I should learn to keep my big fat mouth shut."

Hmm . . . so does that mean she doesn't think I'm a sell-out? Or is she saying she should not have said it aloud? A flügelhorn in my brain is playing off-key. Definite sign of me not quite *feelin'* her apology. Still, I'm just glad for her to be talking to me again. Minus the judgment.

She tells me she liked my photo and post. I tell her I saw. Then she just stares.

And stares.

So I'm like, "Whaaaaaat?"

She gets this joyous, mischievous look in her eyes. She draws in a deep breath and says on a gust of excitement:

"We're going to a school board meeting!"

Seven more boring words have never been spoken. But Rebel's tone makes it seem like she's going to Disney. *"Hey, everybody. I just won the Super Bowl. Guess where I'm going?"*—(dramatic pause)—*"I'm going to a school board meeting!"* It really does sound low-key tragic.

"So," I say, faking my enthusiasm, "a school board meeting? Will there be punch? Games? Fun for the whole family?"

"Ha ha ha," she replies without really laughing.

Then she gets the super intense look in her eyes and says:

"I've been talking with some other kids at MacArthur who're also tired of how the county is treating us. How they don't care about Black kids. We're starting a campaign. Protests, marches, social media—the works. We want to force the county to pay attention to us."

Again, I brace myself. All I can think is, *Uh-oh, she's going to yell at me some more.* I try to picture myself as Dion describes me. It's hard to feel shaken when you're being somebody's muse!

Rebel whips out her phone and shows me a bunch of pictures on social media accounts, #BlackSchoolsMatter and #WakeUpMiamiDade #EducateMe.

I shake out my 'fro like a real muse would. All I can think of is how thoroughly *delighted* our school superintendent will be.

Still, I understand her point. Even agree. We do deserve better schools in our neighborhood. We all deserve the best education possible.

However, a place like the Atlantis School of the Arts is providing me with an outstanding opportunity to get the kind of musical education I could've only dreamed of.

And I am grateful to the school board for making that possible. So it isn't so simple for me to stand up against them.

I don't understand why she always has to make everything a "Black" thing. I mean, I'm Black, too. One look at my bodaciously brown skin makes that clear. But I feel like everybody has a right to a decent school. And traditional schools often treat music education like an afterthought. Would Rebel be fighting for that?

She shows me a tasteful—insert sarcasm here—portrait of a cockroach sunning itself in a midday sunbeam through the grimy cafeteria window at MacArthur Middle.

"Your photography skills have improved, Butterscotch!" Still, I get her point. Conditions at MacArthur aren't great.

Rebel tells me the school board meeting is the next night. Her mom is driving her and a few kids from MacArthur.

Then she tells me what she really, really wants:

"I was thinking, you might be able to come with? Tell them the differences you've seen firsthand. You know? Having

41

grown up in the MacArthur Park neighborhood and now going to the new school."

I get a peach-pit-stuck-in-my-throat type of feeling.

I don't want to go to a school board meeting.

I don't want to cause problems for Atlantis or make it seem like I'm not grateful to have a new school dedicated to the arts.

Excelling at Atlantis so I can convince my dad my skills are good enough to transfer to a private school in Paris would be my dream come true. I'd never get there with MacArthur's curriculum. No way!

I've been stalking one school in particular online since Dad moved. Académie des Arts. It's the equivalent of our middle and high school. It looks amazing, even better than Atlantis. If I haven't mentioned it before, your girl's got plans, man. But . . . it's pricey, and selective. Still, I'm ready to ruffle feathers and put that dream aside. But not if joining the protest means turning my back on Atlantis.

I can't be part of this.

So I tell Rebel a little bit of a lie.

"Mom is making me take a computer class on Tuesday nights. You know, she doesn't want me going to Atlantis any more than you do, but for different reasons. She thinks music is 'not a real job.' Like at twelve I could get a real job." Ha ha ha. Insert laugh track here.

Not a total lie, though. Mom does want me to take a coding class, and it is on Tuesday nights. But not till next week.

No need bothering Rebel with that detail.

Surprisingly, she doesn't explode like she had on Saturday. She knows how Mom can be, so maybe she bought it, which makes me feel a little ill. I don't like lying to her. Rebel used to be the one person I could tell anything.

We walk along in friendly silence, then get back to chitchatting. We're about to reach Sixty-Fourth and separate when she says something that totally stops me.

"Lo, I know we haven't been vibing like we used to, but you're my girl. I'm so proud of you. I think you've worked hard and deserve a great school with new surroundings and all that. I just think . . . the rest of us deserve that, too. Think about it, okay. If not tomorrow, maybe next time. I really need you on my side."

Once again, we go our separate ways.

Rebel has never said she needed me.

But how can I get involved?

Something about protesting the existence of a school that literally answered my prayers doesn't feel right.

Me being there really can't make a difference? *Can it*?

✤

The next night—the night of Rebel's joy-filled school board meeting—Granny comes over for dinner.

As usual, this promises hours of nonstop fun.

Derrick ditched at the last minute. Coward. He knew he was no match for the grandma! And I know he's been ditching out on Mom more and more lately. For someone who is supposedly living with us, he doesn't exactly seem to be *living* with us. What is that about?

Granny walks in with her casserole of doom. A butter-based, noodle-heavy concoction guaranteed to sabotage any dieting goals Mom might have had.

She is the very picture of bitter old lady—tight-curled hair dyed a harsh black; tiny gold-framed glasses that dangle on the tip of her nose; sharp dark eyes able to cut through anyone without warning.

She's a birdlike woman who reminds me of the musical score from an old, old movie composed by Bernard Herrmann called *North by Northwest*. The song is called "The Knife." It's dark and moody and gives me the shivers, but I can't stop loving it. It has highs and lows and drama and range. When I listen to it, I feel the strains of it pulsing inside me, moving like a thief—at first stealthy and measured, then a cacophony, loud and foreboding. That's me and Granny.

Right away she starts singing her greatest hits.

To me: "Chile, when are you gonna let me relax all this beautiful hair? It's time you stopped running around here with your hair sticking out like a pickaninny. And then: "Never heard the word 'pickaninny'? Look it up. It's a HIGHLY derogatory term for a small Black child carried over from slave times." (Thanks, Granny!)

So, to recap, she is basically saying me wearing my

44

natural hair reminded her of baby slaves. *Mmm . . .* can you say "inspirational"?

To my mom, Granny says: "Hmph . . . at least you don't look like you've gained any weight. But you haven't lost any since I saw you last, either. At least, not from what I can tell."

Welcome to Fight Club.

First rule of Fight Club—don't talk about Fight Club!

(Or something like that; I've never seen the movie.)

It takes all my special powers from the ancient gods, me wielding my virtual protective shield—*BING! BANG! POW!*—to repel Mom's and Granny's spears of gloom. It's hard to maintain peace in our home sometimes, especially when she's over.

Granny is so critical of Mom. Always. And she uses her jabs at me as another way of telling Mom, "Your kid is not good enough, either, and it's all your fault." I try not to take it to heart, Granny and her bitterness. I know it's her problem.

My problem is navigating the land mines the two of them scatter for each other.

How do three women opposed to outside conflict create so much conflict themselves?

My job, as always, is to keep smiling, distract both of them with humor and smiles.

I HATE MY JOB.

Granny does that thing she always does when she comes over, looking around the kitchen and sniffing. What is that about?

Then she throws out the first cosmic missile. LET THE OFFENSIVE BEGIN!

She turns to Mom. "Do you use bleach when you clean? I think I smell your second bathroom. You know, back when me and your daddy was raising you and your sisters and brothers, we only had one bathroom. Well, guess it made it easier to keep clean."

Mom glances at me like, "HELP!", so I throw an arm over Granny's shoulder and tell her how wonderful she looks. "I love that cat T-shirt, Granny. You're looking good!"

So lame, I know, but desperate times . . .

At least she changes the subject. But just to start in on my dad.

"How's he doing in Paris? Must be nice. Your father always has been a good-looking man; I bet those French women are throwing themselves at him."

A literal image of Frenchwomen flying through the air, sticking to my dad as though he was some unstoppable magnetic force, is utterly delicious. I giggle, but do my best to hide it because I know this whole conversation topic annoys Mom.

I tell her Daddy is fine.

Me and Mom exchange quick, sneaky glances but say nothing. No need in giving Granny more ammo.

Truth is, I heard from Daddy on Sunday. He'd finally called me back, and I'd been so excited. "I'm so proud of you, baby girl," he said. I had tears of joy in my eyes because it felt good to have at least one of my parents on my side.

We talked for a long while. But later, when I was supposed to be in bed, he called Mom. It didn't take long before the two of them were screaming at each other.

The tears that threatened then were not the joy kind.

Mom had him on speaker because she seems physically incapable of being on the phone any other way. (It makes me sick to my stomach to think she might've done it to let Derrick listen in. My father is none of his business.)

Dad was accusing Mom of not caring about my musical career, and Mom said, "What career? She's twelve, Robert. And you should try steering her to a life that has more stability. Like computer science."

Then Dad laughed, but it was an ugly sound. By that point I was shaking and upset and went back to my room.

I didn't want to tell Granny about him and Mom yelling at each other.

Their divorce was an act of kindness FOR EVERYONE. I just wish they'd be nicer to each other now.

But Granny never runs out of things to be salty about, so next she launches into another one of her tired routines.

Her *Girl, you look so much like your daddy* speech.

". . . the same gorgeous hot cocoa brown skin and eyes so black they sparkle. Yep! Look just like him!" Now, on the surface that always sounds so positive, but DO NOT BE FOOLED.

It is just another way for Granny to beat up on Mom.

Even though me and Mom don't see eye to eye on everything, we're usually cool. We have our things that we do together—Netflix marathons of *America's Next Top Model* or *The Flash*. Our version of fun. At least, when Derrick isn't around.

But she does not like being reminded how much I take after Daddy. It's the same reason she didn't want me to pursue music.

Mom isn't into being artistic anymore. Once upon a time she fell in love with my dad and had the idea of being a potter and sculptor. But . . . it didn't work out that way. And Granny doesn't seem to get the picture that talking about it just makes everything worse.

With our family soap opera, we all have our roles, play our parts. The story and the dialogue are usually the same:

GRANNY:

(to me) "You better count your blessings, Lori Ann. You got your daddy's genes. Nice and thin."

ME:

"Granny!" (My voice super high and playful. A sista knows her lines when it comes to the family dramedy.) "You know my name is Lotus?"

GRANNY:

(snort) "My bad. That's what the kids say,
right. *My bad*."

ME, TO MYSELF:

*Nobody says that, Granny, unless it's to make
fun of people who say it.*

GRANNY:

"You shoulda been named Lori Ann after my
mama. Especially since she left your mama
all that property instead of leaving it to
me, her only daughter. Your mama always
promised me she'd name her first daughter
after Mama—at least, before she ran off and
became a hippie!"

MOM:

"Mother, you know I was exploring my
identity back then. I fell in love with a
musician and artist. I got swept away."

ME:

Internal eye roll. My mom *was* an artist, only
Granny kept telling her she wasn't.

GRANNY:

(double snort) "Your mama got up to FSU
and lost her mind. I sent Willa Jean Carter
to Tallahassee, but when she came back to
Miami Beach she was 'Willow.' Your daddy was
so handsome and smooth talking this chile

changed her name, gave up computer science,
and got a degree in . . . what was that again?
Quilting? Fruit picking?"

MOM:

"Agricultural engineering, Mama, you know
that."

ME:

"They were in love, Granny!" (It's hard to
deliver that line with a straight face! Maybe I
should be in drama, too.)

GRANNY:

"I know what she was in love with all right.
He was a good-looking man and she went head
over heels."

See, here is the thing about my granny:

When my mom and dad got together in college, she had
a fit. "You're not sticking to your plan, Willa Jean Carter."
"You're just throwing away your life, Willa Jean?" "That
man is no good for you, Willa Jean."

On and on, Mama has told me. I wasn't around back
then, of course, but I've heard the stories. Granny loves her
reruns, so over the years she's replayed those early episodes
again and again.

My parents stayed together until I turned seven. I remember Granny going on and on about what a bad father he was;
I remember how much it hurt to hear her say those things.

Soon as they split up, though, and Mom stopped pursuing her art, her life was back on plan—the plan Granny came up with for her life. Mom went back to school, finished a degree program in computer science, got a corporate job. Then Great-Granny died and left Mom some houses that she had rented out in lower-income neighborhoods. And a small apartment building.

Mom didn't let my dad know about all the income she got from those properties, which I thought was downright mean. But . . . I also knew Dad was earning way more money than Mom knew about. Oh, the games people play.

Granny carries on now like my dad is the best thing since sliced bread. However, I know she just wants to ruffle Mom's feathers, whatever choice she made.

(*Fun fact—Sliced bread came to America in July 1928, and at the time people didn't think it was all that great. Sliced bread got stale faster than the uncut loaves people were used to getting at the bakery. But Granny uses that expression, "best thing since sliced bread," all the time.)

I can see Mom turning red, and, out of desperation, I change the subject to the other big thing on my mind.

HUGE mistake.

When you treat parents like grown-ups and share something personal about how you feel, they can really screw it up.

The conversation goes like this:

ME:

"Rebel and some other kids from MacArthur
Park are going to a Miami-Dade County school
board meeting tonight to protest conditions at
all the schools in that district."

MOM:

(Snorts. Some people shrug. Mom inherited
Granny's snort. I pray it isn't hereditary. The
snort stops here!)

ME:

"Rebel asked me to come with, but . . ."

GRANNY:

(viciously shaking her head, cutting me off)
"No, no, no! Don't let Rebel and her rabble-
rousing mamas drag you into being part of
their mess! I've known one of 'em, Eunice's
family, since they were all coming up in the
neighborhood. Eunice raised them girls—
Teresa and Rebel's mama, Janae—to be as
belligerent and stubborn as she was. No good'll
come of it!"

MOM:

(looking uncertain) "You're not planning on
protesting, are you?"

When I say of course not, she visibly sags

with relief. *No standing up to authority for my daughter!* I'm not sure how I feel about that.

MOM:

"I wasn't crazy about you going to a performing arts school, Lotus, but I know for a fact it's a heck of a lot better than our old school. Rundown. Falling apart. They don't care about those kids!"

They.

Those kids.

I hate to say it, but I truly feel a little ashamed of both of them.

ME:

"That's Rebel's point, Mom. I wasn't saying I was going anywhere, just telling you what I was thinking about. Granny asked, remember?"

GRANNY:

(Falling back on a favorite criticism) "Don't get caught up in no mess, hear me? This town is run by the Cubans. A few whites, too. But mostly *the Latins.* Black folks don't matter. Not in Miami Beach." When Granny mentions anyone who isn't Black, she acts like they are to blame for anything bad that happens to Black people. She definitely does not realize she's part of the problem with this attitude.

Or that I have Latina, Black, white and Asian friends at MacArthur and at Atlantis.

Usually, it doesn't faze me when Granny's and Mom's doomsday attitudes are in sync. I go to my room, play music, write songs, wonder about the future and how amazing it might be, and forget all about Fight Club. Me and Rebel video call, and I tell her how impossible Mom and Granny are, and she tells me how impossible her parents are, and then we move on.

But today feels different. Long after Granny leaves and Derrick returns, after I've showered and climbed into bed, the kitchen scene still replays in my mind over and over.

Does Granny really believe that everybody else is out to hold Black people back?

My window overlooks the front porch. Our neighborhood is older, with big trees that've been here forever, curving sidewalks, and roads that twist around roots coming through concrete. Some homes are spruced up, while others are crumbling and look jacked up. A typical block in MacArthur Park.

Wish we had a view of the ocean.

When I grab my violin that night, I play it softly and feel the warmth of the notes caress my cheeks. Johann Sebastian Bach's Partita no. 2, Chaconne, is moody and sad, but hopeful and full of darkness and light. That's how I'm feeling—a jumbled mix of stuff, trying to put the pieces together and figure it all out.

Life has sure gotten harder in seventh.

Like, I ask myself, what does it mean when middle school kids are so frustrated with their school, they're willing to spend an evening fighting for change even when the grownups won't?

And what does it mean when the friends they turn to for help—like me—turn their backs, instead?

Will anyone listen to them?

Would anyone listen to me?

Music had always been close to my heart. But so are my friends.

I can't help but stir up images, remember snapshots in my brain of good teachers at MacArthur, like Mrs. Brown, the one-time music teacher. People who we felt sorry for because they were trying to teach us with nothing. Teachers who probably deserved to be at a "good school."

But you know what?

In all that time, I never once looked around and thought all of us kids deserved better, too. Isn't that funny?

6

The next morning, Maestro is in a mood.

He gets in our faces about goofing off, not being serious enough. Mostly because a lot of kids are talking and goofing off. (I may have been discussing Percy Jackson and *The Lightning Thief* with Tatiana Lee and Anabel, but only for, like, a minute!)

He really rips into me and Tatiana because we are supposed to be "leaders" or whatever. Then we both have to stand and demonstrate proper technique for the piece we are practicing.

Tatiana does pretty well. I do not. At least, he finds every little thing to criticize from my posture to how I am breathing.

I feel squeezed like the bag on a bagpipe. Music is supposed to help me breathe in a way I struggle with at home with Mom and Granny.

Maestro remains relentless, coming at me hard. He says, "If you're not mature enough to handle this responsibility, I can send you back to Mrs. Nan." Wide eyed, I refuse to cry, even though the sting of fresh tears crushes my heart like the highest notes on a violin.

And if that isn't enough, as I'm packing up my case, Adolpho has the nerve to say: "Maestro, can we have a challenge on Friday?"

And Maestro says, "If you feel ready, Mr. Cortez."

A challenge is when an orchestra member in one section or seat challenges another for their spot. Adolpho looks right at me. So not only will I have a vocabulary quiz Friday, but I'll also have to compete for my spot.

All of this is terrible for my chi.

I can't lose my seat to him after only having it for a little bit. What would my dad think?

And then things get worse.

Oh no!

At the end of class when I bend to pick up my music, three paper airplanes tumble out of my hair. Big ones. Soft landings into my violin bag. They must've been stealth planes because I hadn't felt a thing.

I pick them up and turn and say, "Ha ha ha! Like that's never happened before." If anybody's looking, I want to seem like I'm not fazed at all.

I tried to brush it off earlier, but the whole paper-airplane-in-the-'fro business has started to feel quite rude. I mean we aren't in elementary. Who does that? Throw paper planes into someone's hair?

Then, as if things had to get worse, Maestro calls me over. He says I need to be even more focused than the others. He's all, "You have a *gift*, Miss Bloom. When you play, you do so with such passion, such fire. I'm placing a lot of faith in you, believing that you have what it takes to be a fine, disciplined musician. But you are so very young and maybe you are not ready? Are you going to let me down?"

GULP!

No pressure, right?

✿

After school I go to the MacArthur Park Community Center. Run by one of my favorite people in the world—Uncle Stevie.

Seeing Unk is always the best part of my day. He is just That Guy!

So positive. So reassuring.

He loves being a mentor and helping kids—especially the younger dudes. They look up to him because he's a big, athletic Black guy who got educated, even played pro ball for a season, and once was a star offensive lineman at the U.

Now he wants me to volunteer, too. To teach a music class to a group of younger kids.

I agreed. First, because I'd do anything for Unk; and second, because even seventh graders need volunteer service hours. At least, seventh graders at Atlantis do.

But teaching hasn't been like I'd expected at all.

We walk into a small room with six elementary kids sitting around, laughing, throwing little paper wads at one another. My first thought is, *Oh great! More flying paper.*

Unk's voice is like a loudspeaker, so when he says, "Hey! Settle down in here!" the sound booms. The kids are so busted! I know how they feel.

Then Unk introduces me and what he says gives me a shiver.

"Can I have your attention, please. I'd like to introduce you to my niece, a musical prodigy who is so good on violin that she didn't have to audition for that *fancy new school*—she got a special invitation! I want you all to recognize that what she has accomplished is what happens when you put in that work. One of my favorite people on the planet: Miss Lotus Bloom."

The kids actually applaud, and they are totally looking at me like I'm some sort of star. Okay, I low-key feel like I should do the sweeping curtsy move Dion taught me. (Dion has such flash.)

I still don't know what to expect from them. Kids at Biscayne Shores Elementary, my old school, have a rep for being "bad kids." I know not everybody there was "bad." Most of us had been great kids who tried our best to learn even as parts of the ceiling occasionally rained onto our shoulders like plaster dandruff.

But at basketball games or concerts at another school,

you'd wonder if you were going to get treated bad because MacArthur Park kids had such a bad rep.

I don't even have time to worry about any of that because soon as Unk steps aside, questions about Atlantis start:

"Are there any other Black kids there?"

"Do their instruments work?"

"How do you feel going there?"

"Were you scared your first day?"

They are so cute and adorable and thirsty to know more. (I'm at least two years older than most of them! I can call them cute.) I tell them I had been nervous about going there because it wasn't like any school I'd ever dreamed of. And I missed my friends. And yes, there are many other Black students. Although most of the Black kids at Atlantis come from other neighborhoods, other schools. Better schools.

We talk a little more, and after that I play violin for them, then piano.

Four kids want to learn piano; two, violin.

The kids really pay attention, and a few clearly have had some training, a little bit at least. They're trying so hard. I've only just met them and already feel so proud of them. Rebel's voice whispers from my memory:

I think you've worked hard and deserve a great school with new surroundings and all that. I just think . . . the rest of us deserve that, too.

I can't help thinking about Atlantis, where we were issued iPads instead of textbooks and not one single locker has rust on it; where a huge skylight sits above our heads in the cafeteria and it absolutely doesn't leak; where the hallways sometimes felt like a terrarium because of all the plants and sunshine . . . Where we all feel special. Seeing the care they take of the building, how could you not feel how much the administration and teachers value us, too?

It's so weird, because when I was at MacArthur, I was like, *Okay, this is what I'm working with. So bring it on!*

Since going to a different school, a better equipped, more modern building, I realize a school could be so much more than what I was used to.

And that makes me think about Rebel. Why can't it be like that for all schools? Particularly schools with mostly Black kids, like in my neighborhood?

❦

Dad calls at six a.m. on Thursday.

It is noon in Paris. On jeudi—Thursday. (My French is improving. Can't go to school in Paris if I don't know the language, right?)

"Sorry if I woke you," he says.

"I was already up," I reply, letting my smile melt into my words.

"Yoga?"

"Yes, Dad, I am stretched out, chilled out, and ready for my day!" I smile wider when I hear his laugh. I am going to need calm and peace, because every time I think about

61

Adolpho and his challenge I start breathing fast and imagining what it would feel like to—to . . . I don't know. Strike out! Do SOMETHING.

Breathe . . . breathe . . . breathe!

He tells me funny stories about his recent performances. He's in a jazz band and an orchestra—Orchestre de Paris. When I say the name in my head, I can hear Vivaldi's *Four Seasons* playing in my soul. #shivers!

It's so good to hear my dad's voice. I picture him there, dinning in an outdoor café having lunch in the 9th arrondissement. His tall, dark self, seated at an angle so his long legs don't bump the tiny café table. (Though as serious as he is, my father is also a practical joker who loves screwball comedies.)

His French is really good. I totally got a C on my French quiz, but I don't mention that. However, I think he figured that out when he asked, *Comment vas-tu en cours de français, ma chère?* (Thanks to Google, I learned he was asking, "How are you doing in French class, my dear?") and I didn't know how to respond.

He laughs, then tells me he misses me and can't wait to hear me play again in person.

"Your mom ought to be letting you make music and post videos online, ma fille!"

Ma fille. It means "my girl" in French.

Right at that moment I wanted to shout, "Daddy! Come get me! Send for me!" Something. Anything. Right at that moment I wanted to tell him everything—how things are getting complicated here. How I'd researched Académie. How, if he just gave me a chance, I could stay with him and not be a burden.

I've wanted to go live with him in Paris *soooooo* bad. Like really, really bad. And I know how important my music education is to him. But there is one problem:

The tuition is €35,899. That equals 44,959 American dollars! I not only need to get in, I'll need a scholarship, too.

Dad has a secret, too. I figure since he is paying our bills and sending money for me every month, and she had a man living here for free, Mom and Dad are even.

I've been keeping my own, too. I applied for the scholarship and signed both their names.

Okay, I know that getting into the Atlantis School is awesome. And I'm so proud of it. But the school lacks one important thing—it's not in Paris. It's not near Dad. I want to be with him because I know he understands me. He'd never make me feel guilty about wanting a life of music. Not like Rebel. Not like Granny. And not like Mom.

I just haven't exactly asked *him* about it yet.

Heart pounding, a mixture of excitement and hope and fear, I don't even think. I say, "Daddy . . ."

I never call him that, so instantly he knows something is going on. Only I can't get the words out.

I want to tell him what I've done. Truly, I do.

But . . .

"Lotus? Are you having a poor connection?" He brings me back to reality. I can't tell him. Not yet. Once I have the scholarship and the offer, it will be much easier to convince him and Mom that me moving to Paris will work!

Sigh. A poor connection? Yes, Dad, it is.

Not because of internet speeds.

After I come back to my reality, I agree with him that I totally want to upload videos of myself playing, but he knows why I can't.

"Mom thinks if I post videos, I'll get lured into a drug house, or worse, become TikToker scandalous."

Dad laughs because he knows it's true. I feel a little bad for throwing Mom under the bus, but she is really addicted to the idea that one day Mr. Perv would offer me candy in exchange for a violin and I'd just happy-hop my little butt into his van.

Like, really, Mom, really?

Daddy says, "I'll talk to your mom about that again. In the meantime, I've got to split. We're breaking in a new singer this evening. I just hadn't talked to you in a while. My schedule's so busy. Is it okay that I call you at this time?"

"Fine, Dad." I hate feeling like this. I have so much antic-ipation when it comes to hearing from him. But talking to him long distance sometimes feels like a stab in the heart. I really miss him. He and Mom may be divorced, but until he left for Paris, I saw Daddy almost every day. Having him so far away hurts.

"Everything's good? Your mom staying in line?"

"It's all good, Dad. I—I . . . take care, Dad. Call me back tomorrow, okay?"

"I'll try."

7

Not bragging, but on Friday, I crush Adolpho.

CRUSH HIM.

He swaggers up to the front of the room for our challenge. He plays his piece. Technically, he's all right, but he plays like a robot. No soul. I'd have to concentrate really, REALLY hard to play music WITHOUT MOVING!

I don't even look at him. All I keep thinking is no way am I going to lose my spot, not after talking to my dad.

Vivaldi no. 3 in G Major.

My whole soul is in that junk. Flames spring off the strings, and sparkles dance in the air. With quick, brisk strokes, my bow dances across the strings.

The room, Maestro, Adlopho, all fade away. I don't shut my eyes. Instead, my eyes seek out faces I've grown accustomed to. When I smile, they smile in return, moving their bodies to the rhythm same as mine.

That connection is what music is about for me. Feeling something so strongly and being able to share that feeling with someone else.

Maestro says to the room, "Lotus won, would you not agree?"

The class stands and gives me an ovation. Not everyone stands, though.

I wonder if there were any paper airplane pilots sitting in their seats.

For that moment, I don't care.

❧

The second week of school passes, and I'm looking forward to the weekend.

And seeing Rebel.

She comes over Saturday. We walk several blocks along the south end of MacArthur Park, on Eleventh Street. When we get to Washington Street, we walk until we spot my favorite secondhand shop.

I get really hyped when I spot a good sale. Like playing "Summer Madness" by Kool & the Gang, this really old funk band from way back in the '70s. That actor Will Smith sampled it way back when he was a teen rapper, long before I was born. So it's a double vintage vibe. Anyway, it's a super cool tune.

"Look!" I say to Rebel as we reach the rolling rack of dresses. "An authentic psychedelic '70s maxi dress. It is *everything*, for real."

"Definitely goes good with Woolly," she says. Even though it's marked at forty bucks, I'm hoping to talk them down. We walk around, picking up pieces here and there, but I don't dare get anything else. In case I need all my money for the dress.

My bartering skills are on point, and getting the price down to thirty-two dollars makes me feel triumphant. Think Beethoven's *Coriolan Overture*, which is playing in my head.

"I feel like doing something else. Let's go walk around the Art Deco district so I can get some artsy snaps," I say. I love the colorful buildings and funky shapes of homes and businesses there.

"Cool," Rebel says. We're having fun, pitter-patting back and forth about nothing much. Sunshine is hot, but the sea breezes from the bay keep the temps tolerable.

Then, because she can't help herself, Rebel heats things up.

"Don't you think it's pretty wild that back in the '30s, Black folks couldn't walk these streets without an ID card showing that they worked at an area hotel or for a private home?" she says.

Okay, so she's been very good about listening to me and shopping with me. The least I can do is listen to her.

"I didn't know that," I say, which is completely untrue. Granny grew up here, too. She has lots of stories about life here in the "good ol' days." Her stories point out that the good old days were not so good. Not for Black people. I don't share that, though.

"Yep," Rebel goes on. She never looks more pleased with herself than when she's "schooling" you.

"Ordinance 457," she goes on. "It required that Black seasonal workers for the resorts, restaurants, and so on had to report to the police to be fingerprinted and receive special IDs to be able to walk around. And don't get me started on the schools."

Oh god, I really don't want to get her started on the schools. But I know there is no stopping her now.

"Our neighborhood in MacArthur Park only came into being in the mid-'70s. It's where the city 'allowed' Black folks to live. And from the outset, they did little to update the schools beyond the bare minimum. That's why MacArthur Middle is the way it is. We have an obligation to make this right, Lo."

I nod, letting her go with this, and encourage her to join in my selfies in front of a few Art Deco buildings. #ProgressIsPower

"We're going to another meeting next week. You're still invited." She bounces her eyebrows up and down and says it like she's offering me really cool candy.

Or Cheetos.

I decide to come clean. I admit that I can't do it because, if I do, my mom's head will explode. I expect her to go all nuclear on me as usual, but you know what?

She doesn't.

Then comes the biggest surprise ever:

REBEL HAS A BOYFRIEND.

"Not a boyfriend, but a special person who shares my beliefs." That is the Rebel Way of Romance.

Of course, I want to know the deets—gimme all the details, I tell her.

His name is Connor Woods, and he is "an older man," an eighth grader. And he doesn't go to MacArthur. She says he is super political and they don't agree on everything, but he is smart and doesn't make fun of her for being so committed to her causes.

I ask what he looks like. She gets almost defensive.

"Don't get hung up on looks, Lo, that's beneath you." And of course, I agree.

Of course.

Still, I'd never seen *my* Rebel so *ooo-la-la* over some dude. It's nice. And weird. But, yeah, mostly nice.

She has a glow. And that makes me think about Taj, that seventh-grade drummer also promoted to the upper orchestra.

He and I happen to have French together, too. He is Haitian American and African American, and his grandmother speaks French, so he speaks some French at home, and sometimes we say funny things to each other in class.

But I can't imagine talking politics or discussing my innermost ideas or whatever with him. Hmm.

Long after Rebel has left, I am feeling good because we are friends again and talking again and at least for a few hours life is back to normal.

So I have to wonder:

If I did share my innermost ideas or goals or philosophies or world views, what would that look like?

It's one of the things I admire most about Rebel. She always has a clear idea of where she stands and what she believes in. I envy her that gift.

Later that night, a lot of what Rebel said about school segregation replays in my head, even crowding out the music that often fills my thoughts. That rarely happens.

I text her and tell her she has me thinking about things and trying to determine my own life philosophies, and you know what she texts back?

Lotus, you are delightfully adolescent. Don't ever change.

Um, *thank you*?

8

On Sunday, I'm not thinking about philosophies or concertos. I only want to have some fun. I plan to meet up with Dion and Mercedes, as well as two other kids from school, Christian and YaYa, to hang out on South Beach. (Oh, and Taj, too. *Swoon*.)

When you have real dark skin and put on sunscreen, people look at you like you're from another planet, but, hello? Skin is a human organ, and no matter what the shade, it burns. Just 'cause my melanin is on high, don't mean I shouldn't protect my skin, *okaaaaay*?

Meanwhile, Granny stopped by earlier this morning before I left and was kind enough to tell me, "Gal, wear a hat and a coverup. You're dark enough as it is. You'll come back here looking like an eclipse if you get too much sun." Holy colorism, Granny.

Sigh.

Despite that unwanted public announcement—thank you, Granny—the beach is a blast.

Mostly.

Mercedes, who is Cuban, takes her national pride a little far sometimes. She says things about other Latin cultures that aren't so nice.

YaYa, who is Puerto Rican, takes offense. Which is fair. It's awkward because I know Mercedes just likes riling her up!

"Woo! It sure is hot out here, right, Taj?" I say, bouncing my brows up and down.

He smiles. "Sure is, Lotus."

Christian half snorts, half cackles into his hand. "Look, *chicas*," he says to Mercedes and YaYa, "you're frightening the tourists with your culture wars. Bring it down a notch!"

I try not to look at him. Then we both burst out laughing, anyway!

Here I am, sitting under my floppy hat on a beach towel. I have a fresh bag of Cheetos and an icy Coke, earbuds and a killer playlist.

And the Atlantic Ocean. Why ruin that chill?

Eventually, they all calm down and then we take a bunch of selfies and I dare to get into the ocean and allow the woolly mammoth to get wet. It's wash day for my hair, anyway, since we have Monday off for Labor Day. In most civilized parts of the country, school doesn't start until after Labor Day, but not good ol' Florida. We're already knee-deep in the nonsense!

Now, when we get out of the water, Taj asks me about the paper airplanes and balls of paper that keep mysteriously landing in my hair. Which is another decidedly un-chill topic. But it would be good to know what he thinks.

"Do you know who's doing it?" he says. "I think for sure Adam Benito, one of Adolpho's friends, is one of the, er, *pilots*."

Mercedes pipes in, "I heard something about you, too, mami!" Mercedes calls everyone "mami" or "chica." "Papi," too.

"Moi?" Instead of sounding exotic and carefree, my words come out like a croak. (Gotta practice that French, right?) Mercedes isn't even in orchestra, so somehow this news has spread.

She says she heard some girls talking about how mad Adolpho was that he got booted from first-chair violin and how he wants to *"make her suffer."* Meaning me.

YaYa jumps in, as if the whole argument with Mercedes is forgotten, and says, "I'm not in orchestra, either, obviously, but if I were you, I'd report it. You shouldn't let them get away with that!"

Mercedes agrees "Definitely, mami! You need to check him before it gets out of hand. Not your fault that when it comes to violin, you're the Baddest B."

"Shut up!" yells YaYa. "What do you know about it, anyway?"

"I know you're not even . . ."

74

Dion cuts Mercedes off, breaking into a soliloquy:

"So full of artless jealousy is guilt,
It spills itself in fearing to be spilt!"

It should be weird, but it's kind of adorable.

"That's from *Hamlet*, character the Queen," he says, giving us mad doses of Billy Porter.

Christian rolls his eyes. "Leave it to you to speak for the queen!"

We all laugh, and Dion dips into a savage curtsy. Then he stands, looks me in the eye, and says, "Look here, girl, you need to stand up for yourself. Turning the other cheek . . . that might work in the Bible, but Jesus never went to middle school."

All I want is for this to blow over. But I'm afraid he might be right.

☙

By the time I get home, I feel beat down by the sun and tired from swimming (and all the chitchat).

Mom agrees to help me wash my hair. Yes, there are Insta photos—#TameTheMammoth #AfroDown.

She is in a good mood. Derrick is gone, so it's just the two of us, like the good old days. Her making fajitas for dinner and both of us chilling, sitting around, watching old black-and-white movies—her favorite—as she detangles my hair and twists it up.

Tonight we're watching something called *Casablanca*. Mom says it's a classic that always makes her cry. Black-and-white movies sort of freak me out, but this one turns out to be pretty good. They keep playing this one song over and over, and the main guy—Mom calls him "Bogie," short for Humphrey Bogart—keeps telling the Black dude on the piano to "play it again, Sam."

It is a little trippy, but all in all, not bad.

But what keeps me awake later is the conversation I have with my mom when the movie ends.

I'd been thinking about all the stuff my new friends talked about at the beach.

I tell Mom how weird it was to hear people saying stuff like that and challenging one another, and how I don't agree with it but also don't know if it's my place to step in. Then, after thinking about it a little more, I tell her about the paper airplanes.

"Mercedes and YaYa think I should say something to our teacher or somebody. Do you think so?"

Mom gets real still—like statue still. "Mom? You all right? Did you hear what I said?"

She nods, then she says, "Lotus, don't make waves. You're not going to die because of a few paper airplanes landing in your hair. You're tougher than that."

I want to tell her it isn't about being tough.

I want to tell her it has been going on almost since the first day of school and I *haven't* made waves about it. But that it's starting to get to me.

I want to tell her how I am not scared, just sort of annoyed. It's disrespectful.

But now she's looking down at the floor. When she looks up, she gives me this weird smile, like she's trying to make everything better, only she just doesn't know how.

And what she says isn't better at all. "You're so thin and pretty, that boy probably just has a crush on you. He'll tire of messing with you soon and move on to someone else. Boys— men—always do."

Mom's own self-esteem always comes back to that— being attractive. Like as long as a girl is pretty, nothing else matters.

I remember Granny one day holding up a framed photo of Mom at her high school graduation. I thought Mom looked gorgeous, but Granny said, "I sure wish that girl could've lost a few pounds before the ceremony. My friends were there from out of town!" I guess I know where those feelings came from.

Now Mom is going on about how nice it must be to look a certain way, and don't I feel lucky and blessed. And just like that, I am not even sure we are talking about me at all.

❧

It's not unusual for me to wake in the middle of the night at four a.m. Only this time I can't fall back asleep.

That conversation burns in my chest like the fajita peppers. I wish I could take some Pepto and make it all go away.

77

Except my mom's voice, soft and singsongy, keeps replaying in my head.

Her message is clear:
• Stay quiet.
• Don't fight back.
• Don't make trouble.

Hmm . . . ?

Mom is like the anti-Rebel.

So much is going on in my head. I don't know what to do with it.

I take out my violin and, soft as I can, play Bach's *BWV 1001: II. Fugue*—its melody is lovely and soothing, and it moves gently through me, wrapping my spirit in warm hugs.

It does make me feel better; even though I still don't have an answer for any of my many questions about life. The sonata replays in my head, long after I lay down my violin and go to sleep.

9

Our performances at the high school and open house are only a few weeks away, and Maestro is being a total beast.

He's barking at us like we have a performance tomorrow. Maybe I can talk to him about breathing deep from his belly. Woo-saaah! It's a great way to relax.

Sigh. Probably not a good idea to tell Maestro to chill.

It's only been a few weeks, but I am learning a lot from him. My pacing and technique and the quality of sound from my instrument have all improved.

The biggest lesson I learned:

No excuses!

He expects results. Period.

When school first started, I felt awestruck every day. The high atrium; clean bathrooms, with soap dispensers with soap in them; the way the staircase in the main hall swoops and curls like frosting on a cupcake—it was all so amazing.

Now, three weeks later, who has time for architecture?

The pressure of the upcoming performances is getting too real. Me, Tatiana—Tati now that we've become friends—and Anabel are working with the other members of our section, making sure everyone understands how to do their fingering, when to apply more rosin, the best way to hold the neck of the violin.

As first chair, I'm responsible for how we work together. I am definitely feeling more stressed. I wonder how much yoga I'll have to do to release and relax.

It still freaks me out that I'm younger than almost everyone here. Most of my classmates at least listen to my advice.

Most, but not all.

The paper airplane attacks have grown more regular—as in every other day—but I'd decided to keep it to myself. Maybe Mom was right. Maybe I'll be better off if I don't make a fuss.

But now it's the end of the week and I'm sort of exhausted.

Right as class is ending, I bend to pick up my case, and— ZING!—paper airplane right in the face!

My competition looks right at me. So far, I've only caught his minions in the act; this is the first time he's been so obvious about it.

"Real mature, Adolpho," I say. He rewards me with a hand gesture I'd rather not decipher.

Tatiana clearly caught it, too. "How much more of this are you going to put up with before you do something about it?"

She mirrors me—violin bag strap over one shoulder, bow in hand. I swing around and finish packing away my instrument.

"No need to make a big deal out of it." I say it nonchalantly, like I'm not dragon-fire mad. I want to believe it'll all be fine. I want Mom to be right.

But one look at the expression on Tati's face and I know better.

"It's not okay, Lotus. And it won't get better by itself," she says. But she seems to give up on me with a sigh. "Later."

We go our separate ways, and I try not to obsess over the ridiculousness of Adolpho Cortez and his henchmen.

I might not be comfortable with conflict, but as a born-in-April Taurus, I have more than my share of stubbornness. Let him throw his paper balls and planes. It'll makes me work that much harder to prove I am better than him no matter what he does.

For now, I do nothing. Like Mom said, I can handle it. Right?

❧

I might be getting use to the utterly space-age bathroom with its automatic lights, the super cool electronic whiteboards, and the hallways cleaned hourly, but I am still in awe of the cafeteria. Or *café*, with fresh food stations instead of unrecognizable piles of sloppy joe or square-shaped pizza. Rather, we have fresh, handmade pizza slices sitting in shiny steel-wheeled carts with small awnings atop them. It is set up like a food court in an old-fashioned town square.

My usual is pasta with garlic toast points. I can smell actual fresh spices. The scent spirals upward and tingles my skin. All of a sudden, I feel weak-kneed with hunger.

At lunchtime, Mercedes is holding court, as usual. She talks fast, more animated than ever.

She and YaYa and Taj are often part of my lunchtime posse. Sometimes Dion joins us, but mostly he doesn't. I don't think Dion cares much for Mercedes. I figure the wattage of their combined big personalities clashes.

All the cliques around the sun-filled room are super amped today. I see how hard Mercedes fights for a starring role—Cafeteria Diva, and all that. Well, she is in theater. She, along with all the other departments, is in performance mode, too.

Today she tells me she is really feeling my vintage vibe. My authentic '70s granny skirt with a hand-crocheted tank is killer, if I do say so myself. And I do. Low-rise leather ankle boots. Bright yellow silk flower in my hair. Yeah. It's a look.

"I love how cool you look with the flowers in your *woolly mammoth*," she says, and everybody laughs. I'd clued them all in to my 'fro's social media stardom. When she says, "woolly mammoth," it whooshes between her lips with the exultant lift of a saxophone note.

"Where do you find such unique outfits?" YaYa asks.

I inhale a forkful of pasta. "Secondhand shops around the area. Sometimes a few of the Lincoln Road stores carry neat, authentic finds."

Talking about style is a nice distraction from the craziness going on in my life. And it feels good to have Mercedes always so enthusiastic about my look. But sometimes I feel like she's messing with me. Like, I don't want to be negative, but sometimes her compliments don't feel sincere.

Is middle school making me jaded? That's so not me.

The two of them dive into other conversations. I try to steady my breathing when Taj's knee brushes mine under the table.

Did I mention his total, undeniable hotness? I did, didn't I?

Finally, I stop drooling long enough to notice something else—some*one*.

Off to one corner of the room, a girl is sitting alone. A Black girl with long braids. Maybe African American or Haitian or even Panamanian. Living in South Florida teaches you never to assume. Just because someone is brown doesn't mean they're African American.

"Mercedes, do you know her?" I ask, gesturing to the girl, who appears to be a sea of calm amid all the noise and social drama.

"Visual arts. Boring. I think her name is Farrah, Fabiola, something," Mercedes says. The way she dismisses the girl with a toss of her pretty head and swingy hair bothers me.

That nagging feeling returns—the one that's making me believe my new friend isn't the friend I thought. Then, of course, I can't help thinking about Rebel. I wonder what she's doing at this exact moment.

A little smile moves from my brain to my lips as I picture Rebel in our old cafeteria. Probably sitting with Monique Calvin and Tres Bryant. We used to hang with them a lot. Monique is funny. Tres, that boy's a trip. He likes to fight the power as much as Rebel, but I think he cares more about fighting with whoever is in charge than fighting for people's rights.

Then my smile slips. Because now I'm comparing their lunch experience to mine—shabby, yellowed walls with peeling paint versus the café's crisp white walls with framed art; windowsills littered with dust, crushed milk cartons, and sunbathing bugs versus a wall of floor-to-ceiling glass that opens into a garden courtyard.

I feel a lump rise in my throat and fight desperately to push it down.

Mercedes's laugh brings my attention back to the moment. After stealing another glance at the girl eating alone, I jump into the conversation at our table.

We spend the rest of lunch with our voices rising over one another's about trends and music. A totally chill vibe.

But I can't shake the image of Rebel and our other friends. I wish they were here.

Feeling bold, I find an excuse to leave the lunchroom early and sneak my phone out. I manage to find a spot in the dead-zone terrarium-bowl hallway where I get a signal. I check Rebel's Instagram—@blkgirlsunity.

She'd just posted, like, a minute earlier.

The photo shows Rebel standing next to some dude, leaning into him. Both are holding up the peace sign. They are clearly in the cafeteria at MacArthur, same table me and Rebel and our squad used last year. The caption reads:

Do you know who you are?
#fightthepower @ProudBlackAngel @MalcolmNEXT
#education #Fixourschool

I can't believe my eyes.

Her boo is a WHITE dude.

Nothing wrong with dating a white guy. I never think about stuff like that. But Rebel? Miss Black America, all Black, all the time Rebel?

The way he is looking at her, the way she is leaning into him, this has to be Connor Woods. Of course, reading the tag—@CWood4life—is one big fat clue.

Rebel is kicking it with this guy I don't even know. How did we get here?

I chew inside my lip and drop my phone back into my

bag. A knot forms in my chest, a stone pressing into my heart—a longing for the way things used to be.

And the cold realization that they will never be again.

❧

I awake in the middle of the night still thinking about Rebel and Connor. Battling corruption in the world. Standing up for people's rights. Asking questions.

Do you know who you are? #TimetoSpeakUp

It makes me wonder:

Who am *I*?

❧

The next afternoon in Miss Jackson's class, she discusses our upcoming project due at the end of the marking period.

"Class, we are reading *I Know Why the Caged Bird Sings*." I feel my insides groan. My fifth-grade teacher tried to get me to read that book. I tried. I really did. But it was all about this poor Black girl growing up after the Great Depression in the Deep South.

I got bored just looking at it.

One girl in our class—some of us call her "four-point-oh Franny"—is quick to stand up and give her latest soliloquy on literature. Like anybody asked her to throw in an opinion.

"Miss Jackson, I read Maya Angelou's classic tale of silent protest years ago. I'm really looking forward to reading it again," she says.

86

She is a living, breathing ad for milk. Milky white skin sprinkled with strawberry freckles. Her brown hair in two swishy ponytails. She looks like the star of a Hallmark movie about puppies—and true love!

"Yes, thank you, Franny," Miss Jackson says, not sounding thankful at all. Several of us try hard and mostly fail at holding our laughter on the inside.

Franny, as usual, fails to notice.

Miss Jackson explains our project. It sounds monumental. Sometimes it's hard for me to remember I have classes other than orchestra.

"You will pair Angelou's seminal literary work with the factual history of the Great Migration between 1915 and 1960 when over three million African Americans moved north in search of a better life," she says.

More groans. Eye rolls. Expressions of doom and despair.

Diego something or other—a visual arts students from the other side of the planet as far as I'm concerned—wails, "Miss Jackson, can't we save this for Black History Month or something? Why do we all . . ."

The lang arts teacher cuts him off.

"Look here," she snaps. "I know you are not about to ask me why we all are studying Black history—even those of us who aren't Black. Every month features white history. During the rest of the school year, your literature and history teachers are going to team up to study the history of Japanese, Cuban, Irish, Chinese, and Jewish Americans, and all the other peoples and cultures that worked to make this country what it is."

Sometimes when Miss Jackson breaks it down for you, you feel it in your gut. She does not mess around.

Our history teacher, Mr. Burke, begins speaking. (Miss Jackson and Mr. Burke share our space. The two teachers work as one unit, teaching lang arts and history, and sometimes combining them.) He tells us we'll be studying social revolutions and rebellions that changed society, and sometimes the world.

An electric zap singes my soul. I feel like I'm on a hidden-camera show.

Revolutions?

Where is Rebel when I need her?

Mr. Burke starts talking about the other revolutions, and my brain drifts into me playing *La Campanella* on the guitar. (I love guitar solos.)

But Mr. Burke's enthusiasm brings me back. He's telling us stories that are entertaining, talking about the American Revolution like he's an insider, like he's been hanging with old George Washington at Ye Olde Pub getting the four-one-one along with Thomas Paine and John Adams. (Those were real people, right?)

He tells us that the American colonists didn't start out trying to break completely from the British, wanting only to have the protection of the crown, but old George (King George to those of you who didn't hang with him like Mr. Burke did) got a stick up his butt and decided, *Off with their heads.* (Don't quote me on that last part.)

Mr. Burke says, "Rebellions happen when people get fed up with the status quo. Can any of you name an example of a time when you got fed up with the status quo and decided it was time to do something about it?"

Rebel.

That girl is all about fighting the status quo and all the quos. Meanwhile, I've always thought stepping back and not getting worked up about the status quo was the way to go.

Mr. Burke's voice cuts into my thoughts. "After you read Maya Angelou, you can choose three areas of the Northern migration to research:

"First, you can create a timeline of American history during the time of Miss Angelou's memoir. The timeline must include facts of interest from government as it pertains to laws governing African Americans at that time.

"Second, if you are artistic, you can make your own graphic novel depicting key points in history during the time of the literary work.

"Or third, you can submit your own creative idea that you can pursue upon approval."

I look around. Fun-fact Franny is busily scribbling in her notebook.

Thank goodness no one else is taking notes because I'm not, either. It is hard focusing on any of it.

I keep thinking of my upcoming orchestra deadlines.

The performance at Freedom High's football game. The open house. And of course, the holiday concert.

Will I be ready in time?

"Miss Bloom? Did you hear what I said?" I look up to see Mr. Burke standing over me. The J sisters—Jordan and Janelle, not real sisters—are looking my way, laughing.

"Lotus, you were daydreaming when Mr. Burke asked if . . . ," begins four-point Franny before the teacher cuts her off.

"I've got this, Francis," he says before turning back to me. "You seem distracted today. Everything okay?"

Even though my cheeks don't glow red when I'm embarrassed, I feel the heat.

"Sorry, sir," I mumble.

His smile is kind, understanding even. I manage to exhale and return my own. He says, "I was telling the group to think about pairing up with a partner. Any ideas?"

Thank god he looks at my pitiable smile and decides to walk away.

Suddenly, I feel TOTALLY overwhelmed—by everything.

I just need to make it through the football pregame performance. If I can do that, I'll have a chance to work with the whole orchestra, get them feeling the music, and we'll be fine.

I'll be fine.

10

The rest of the next two weeks fly by in a jumble of reading assignments, writing assignments, and math equations. On top of that, orchestra rehearsals shift to three nights a week. Mom doesn't understand why I'd want to spend even more time at school, but I tell her it's important.

By the time performance Friday arrives, we are all hyper, amped, and super ready for a real audience. The evening starts out full of excited nerves and fun. We ride on a bus, which Taj calls the "Cheese Box," and I sit with Tatiana, Anabel, and a few other violinists. We play music on the bus, act silly, blow off steam. It's so awesome.

Adolpho does a lot of glaring and sneering, like he was president of the International Sneering Committee. *Whatever, dude! You can't dull my shine.* I put him in my hater file and sit back, playing my violin with loose abandon until we arrive.

Purple stripes of sky piped with deep magentas and swirls of orange form a painting of twilight glory. The air tastes faintly of ocean air and grilled hamburger smoke. A perfectly delicious night for a football game.

It is the first home game, and kids thread into the football stadium decked out in bright red and white tees over every shade of denim in the rainbow.

I shut my eyes for a moment of meditation. All we have to do is get through three and a half minutes of a relatively easy piece. I used to like having Rebel in the crowd to cheer me on whenever I played. Now our schedules bump up against each other's, twirling in opposite directions like bumper cars. I miss her.

I try to FaceTime Dad from the field, but he doesn't pick up. I didn't really expect him to. If it's six o'clock in the evening here, it's midnight in Paris.

When I spot Dion at the railings in the bleachers, I run over and ask him to record our performance.

"Girl, you know I'm here for you!" he says. Then I follow his eyes over to a group of high school guys flexing and flossing, and throw him a look.

"Oh, no, baby boy, you're not here for *me*!" I laugh.

"Okay, maybe not *only* for you!" His laughter follows me back to my chair on the edge of the field. Maestro began signaling for us to assemble.

Tatiana leans over and whispers, "Are you ready for this?"

A shiver dances across my skin and through my body. I nod. "Think so," I say quietly. Then it's time to do what I do. "Come on, Tati," I say, gathering my nerves, "let's get everybody tuned up."

I feel Maestro's eyes on us but try not to look at him. I focus, instead, on moving through the violin section, making sure everyone's instrument is on pitch. Tatiana helps. When we get to the area where Adolpho is seated, I exhale slowly.

A kid in the high school's marching band blows a loud note on his tuba. It drowns Adolpho out, which suits me just fine. But I am close enough to read his lips. "Don't even think you can tell me what to do," he growls.

"Well, if you're out of tune, that's between you and Maestro," I say, and keep moving. I feel my heart rate speed up but force myself to push past it.

"This is the toughest part of the night," I say to myself. "You'll only have to deal with him for three minutes, then you're home free."

By the time Maestro introduces us, a bass drum is pounding in my chest so hard I can barely hear.

Still, somehow, I manage to follow his cues and hit my marks. I have a small solo in the piece, then it is over.

"We did it!" I squeak to Tatiana.

"Hey, ho; hey, ho!" Tati rocks side to side, and I giggle out a thousand pounds of stress, feeling a weight life off me. For the first time tonight, I'm truly enjoying myself.

"Let's get hot dogs!" Anabel says as we make our way off

the field and into the concessions area. On the loudspeaker, a man starts talking about the Freedom High School Patriots, and there's a roar from the crowd.

We find hot dogs and chow down. There's something so magical about being here. Slowly, I let the drama of the past several weeks wash off me. I'm okay. I'm better than okay.

Dion comes up and shows me the recording he shot.

"Thank you!"

"I had to use my panoramic view to get you and all that hair in the shot!" he says.

I'm laughing so hard that I snort. The wind had caused the 'fro to sway gently to its own beat. I grin.

"Send it to me," I say. "I want to post it."

Right away, the video gets a like. Rebel. I write:

Wish you were here

I tag Dad, but he doesn't respond, so I put my phone away. We've been talking more regularly lately, so I know I'll hear from him tomorrow.

The night is going so well, I don't even think about any of the things that had me so stressed.

Like Mom not wanting me to be in orchestra, then not wanting me to do anything that could get me kicked out of Atlantis.

Like Adolpho hating my guts, or my fear that I don't have enough time for my other studies outside of orchestra.

With only a few minutes left in the game, it's finally time to pack up and go home. I need to grab some things out of the music locker room.

The lockers for band and orchestra are slightly underground. I'm on a narrow staircase leading into the music bunker. That's when I bump into him again—Adolpho.

He's coming up the steps toward me. He whispers, "You're such a joke. You look ridiculous with that hair!" Then he pushes past me.

He's so *angry*.

I hate myself for feeling tears in my eyes. But I don't cry.

And I don't tell anyone, either.

I *can* continue to ignore him, like Mom said. I really can. Besides, backing off beats fighting with him. What good would it do, anyway?

☸

But as the next few days pass, it's as if I can feel time tick-tick-ticking away. Somewhere deep inside me, a kettle drum booms its throaty rhythm.

It's the last week of September, about five or six weeks before the holiday concert—a week before open house—but already I'm feeling behind.

☸

Thank goodness I don't play a wind instrument. Lately, I'm finding it hard to breathe. Especially when I think too much. Which is more and more lately.

Like I can't stop thinking about how the whole paper-airplanes-in-my-'fro situation is getting old. Like ancient.

And how Mr. Burke and Miss Jackson scheduled the due date for the big, super boring project for two weeks after the open house.

And I can't stop repeating the question on Rebel's social media:

Do you know who you are?

Who am I? I'm a combination of musical notes, of strings and horns and drumbeats that start in my chest and radiate through my eardrums, down my body and into my joints, my limbs, my toes.

I am . . . what? A musician. A girl. An afro-rocking diva. Is that enough?

Another word steals into my thoughts and ruins my appetite for breakfast. It casts shadows on my walk to school, where Rebel fails to miraculously appear as she'd done the week before. The word whispers into my ear, then into my brain. I want to bat it away like a mosquito, but it won't leave.

Coward . . . buzzzzz-coward . . . buzzzzz-coward.

Orchestra is mercifully fast paced. Maestro even manages to say something nice about our weekend performance at Freedom, though I'm already thinking about the music I'll need to memorize for open house.

"You okay?" Tati asks. I shrug at her, unwilling to talk about Friday night's snarl-fest with Adolpho.

"I'm all right," I lie. I make a point of not looking in Adolpho's direction.

At least today, when orchestra ends, no more paper missiles land in my hair. I'm looking forward to going to lunch, getting distracted from this particular drama.

The eighth and ninth graders are away for the day, so we seventh graders have the lunchroom to ourselves. We don't have to worry about being judged and are able to go wild—well, performing-arts-school wild. (There will be no trash can fires or pyrotechnics, and no Shakespearean texts will be harmed in the making of this jam.)

Taj and a few other percussionists are on drums, and Mercedes is on the xylophone. YaYa's singing has even the cafeteria ladies swaying. When I first got here, I'd been amazed that they kept a piano and other instruments set up in here.

As the rhythm hums beneath the tiles and pulses into the soles of our feet, the roundness of butts in chairs, the smiles that spring up like miracles, kids from dance practice their routines, too. It's an open house preview.

Dion is killing it on piano. He's good, especially for someone actually studying visual arts. And the strings—oh, baby, I've got that violin smoking. It's all fire.

When we finish and heartily applaud ourselves (with all the humility of a group of performing arts students), I spot that girl again. I haven't seen her in a few weeks. Now she's here. Same spot. Still by herself.

My curiosity takes over.

"Hi," I say, walking over. "My name is Lotus Bloom."

She gives a crooked grin, "I know who you are, Lotus Big-Time Violinist Bloom."

"Wow! I didn't know I had a title," I say, smiling, and sigh with relief when she smiles back.

"I'm Fabiola French," she says. Her words have a slight tilt, same as her dark eyes. Haitian? Colombian? West Indian? Ahh, the beauty of South Florida—anyone could be from anywhere. Don't you dare try to guess, because you might get your feelings hurt.

"You know, anytime you want to come over, you're welcome at our table," I say.

"I will give *you* that same invitation. I'm not really eager to sit with Miss Mercedes. You should be careful, as well," she says. I take her in and realize that up close, she isn't what I was expecting. Rather than seeming shy and quiet, her eyes spark with energy. An almost daring quality behind the brightness, while her tone is soft but assured.

However, her dark-eyed gaze is steady and confident. So steady, in fact, that it makes me a little uncomfortable. I feel like she's looking into my soul.

"What do you mean?" I ask, still trying to smile, but feeling it sag with uncertainty. "You don't like Mercedes? I know she can seem a little extra, but she's cool."

"I've known her a while. Be careful. She is a backstabber, and the minute she can, she will turn on you," she says. "You seem like a nice girl. I've seen you around. I'd like to hang out sometime. It's just that I know Mercedes from way back. I've seen how she operates. Watch out for yourself and try not to get burned." Her voice is calm, level. She doesn't appear angry. Actually, the opposite. A smile settles into her eyes, and she stands to dump her tray.

From across the room, Mercedes calls out to me. I glance back at Fabiola, feeling more than a little unsettled. Mercedes calls out again.

"Okay," I say with a noncommittal shrug, "well, it was nice meeting you, Fabiola."

"You, too, Lotus Bloom. Take care of yourself. Remember, anytime you need to switch tables you are welcome to join me."

The way her dark eyes scan me, like a cyborg checking out my internal hardware system, further unnerves me. Yet the vibe I got off her was friendly.

Back at my usual table, everyone appears super hyped for our upcoming performance. I'm digging the mood . . . until YaYa turns to me and asks, "So, chica, what have you done to Adolpho Cortez to make him hate you so much?"

She's sucking on a Blow Pop, the candy painting her lips bright red. Her long, dark brown hair is swept to one side, scraped back from her face into a ponytail, held with an elastic band.

"I don't have a problem with him," I lie, not exactly meeting her eyes. "If he has a problem with *me*, you should ask him what it is."

"Well, he posted something about you on Snap." She opens her phone and shows me a screenshot of a post.

It's a meme, a black-and-white image, old fashioned, of a Black boy with wild hair. His eyes are bugged out, and the caption says, "Oh tay!" Adolpho has written:

"When you lose your orchestra seat to Buckwheat, you be like . . ." and then the image zooms in, making the whites of the little boy's eyes big as dinner plates.

"What the . . . ," I say, because I don't know what else to say.

A few kids, Mercedes included, snort as they try to hold back laughter. I am not laughing. It is humiliating. I feel violated.

YaYa pipes in, as always. "I'm not sure who or what a Buckwheat is, but, girl, it just don't feel right. Adolpho is being shady, that's all I've got to say!"

"That's messed up, girl. He's just super salty because he lost his seat to you," says Mercedes. I glance at her and can't help but feel like her concern is a little more fake. Like she's laughing at me but trying to hide it. Is what Fabiola said getting to me? Mercedes adds, "Don't even worry about it."

But . . .

I am starting to worry about it.

That image feels so . . . degrading. Was this Buckwheat a real person or some kind of movie character? I'm not sure.

I tell myself to breathe.

I tell myself not to let this get to me.

I tell myself it will all be worth it when I win that scholarship and move to Paris with my dad.

I want to believe that so much.

But still . . .

When I google "Buckwheat" on my phone and see that character comes from an old TV series, like way, way, WAY back in the 1930s, I also find all these reviews, articles, and critiques about America's history of being entertained by Black characters with exaggerated reactions, messed-up hair, and other stereotypical qualities.

The series was called *Our Gang*. And the Buckwheat character, with his wild spidery 'fro and his wide-eyed expression, is the exact image of what my granny means when she calls me a pickaninny.

It is awful. Way worse than I'd pictured.

Then I go to YouTube. Buckwheat is portrayed as ignorant and simple. It makes me sick to my stomach. I can't fake away my feelings with forced smiles and "what evs."

Buckwheat knocked all the pretending right out of me.

11

Rebel stops by the rec center after I finish volunteering.

I'm in the music room. I've had the little kids doing this musical exercise where they dance around to a rhythm. They loved it, but now loose-leaf music sheets and worn music books clutter the floor. Volunteering is hard work!

"Saw your post today," I say.

"Yeah, me and Connor were . . ."

Then for, like, the next half hour it's "me and Connor" this and "me and Connor" that.

She says that even though he goes to Freedom Middle, he is helping her organize the MacArthur group's trip to the school board meeting tomorrow.

"He's committed," she says. "What about you? Sure you don't want to come?"

I'm putting away instruments that have been donated. I cringe inwardly at how shabby they all are. Especially compared with Atlantis's. Then I cringe again for thinking that way.

"Can't," I say, distracted, already mentally listing out the elaborate array of pre-poo, deep conditioning, and twistups I'll conduct when I get home, to make sure my hair is the best it ever looks at school tomorrow.

The real excuse I give isn't even a lie. "We have late orchestra practice every night this week. Our open house is coming up." For one second we lock eyes, and the urge to spill my guts is so strong I want to cry out.

But I don't.

Instead, I look away and tell myself getting Rebel involved will likely lead to making me do something I'm not comfortable with. Like reporting Adolpho.

Using all her supernatural friend power, she puts her hands on her hips and glares at me.

"Something else is up with you. I can tell," she says.

"No it's not!" I say . . . in a tone that reveals there *absolutely* is something wrong. I blow out a sigh. "I'm just so overwhelmed with the workload at school. Between that and extra practices, I'm sort of going crazy."

She seems to accept it. Or maybe now that she has Connor, she doesn't even miss me!

I can't see her face because of my wall of hair. Also, I'm a little ashamed of how petty I'm feeling. That whole Buckwheat thing is in my head. That awful meme.

Is that really how people see me? Do they look at my hair—which I love—as something dirty and unkempt?

I get down on the floor to collect the music books that the kids left behind. When I finally look up, I see her staring at me. I frown.

"What?" I ask.

She cocks her head to one side and gives me a curious stare. She says, "I'm wondering what's really up with you."

"Nothing," I say, much too quickly.

"*Hmm . . . ,*" she says.

"Miss Lotus," a voice calls from the doorway. We both turn and see two kids coming with two adults. The kids I recognize. They're my little students. But the grown-ups, I'm not sure.

Then Unk comes in behind them.

"Hey, Mr. Knight!" Rebel gives my uncle a hug.

"Rebel with a cause!" he says, like he always does when he sees her. "Good to see you here. Lotus, this is Amya Hurd, Drake's mom."

The woman smiles. "How do you do?" she says.

"And," Uncle continues, "this is Joe Town, Ava's granddad."

I stand. Drake and Ava are two of my most talented students.

The grandfather, Mr. Town, is hickory dark, wearing a slick hat and perfectly shined shoes. He reaches out his hand. "Hello, young lady. How you doing?" His smile is warm, and his teeth are white and even. I can't help smiling back, feeling some of the tension from earlier evaporating.

"Hi, sir. I'm fine. Hi, Mrs. Hurd," I say to Drake's mom.

"It's *Miss*," she says. "I'm not married." She looks pretty young, even though I know Drake is ten.

Rebel, sensing I need a moment, says her goodbyes. "Lotus, I'll check with you later, maybe after the school board meeting. 'Bye, everybody!" She waves and heads out the door.

"The school board meeting?" Uncle asks.

"She's trying to get the school board to put some more money into our—I mean, MacArthur Park—schools."

"Good for her!" Mr. Town says, his sharp eyes flashing with interest. "Are you fighting for some kind of music program for those kids, too?"

I feel the heat of shame seep into my cheeks as he assumes I'm involved in Rebel's cause. We're all standing around in this back room at the center, which is clean and well stocked despite its shabbiness. The center could use a total refurbishment. Still, it's a hundred percent better than MacArthur Middle or Biscayne Shores Elementary.

Suddenly, I feel hot and tired and even more irritable. I don't want to be here, with one more stressful thing on my mind that I don't know what to do about—don't know if I *should* be doing anything about. I want to leave and go away and not go home and not wonder if my father is going to call or whether or not I'm going to turn around and have a dozen paper airplanes tumbling out of my hair.

I just want to make everything stop for, like, five minutes. Just stop.

But as the thought pushes around inside my head, I feel them all looking at me. I feel little Ava—the sweetest little thing—grab hold of my fingers. She loves piano and has such a pretty singing voice for someone so young.

"Miss Lotus, I just wanted you to meet my pop-pop." Then she wraps her arms around me, and I feel myself hold my breath, afraid I'll start to cry.

What is wrong with me?

Uncle's smile beams. He looks from me to Mr. Town and says, "Lotus has been an excellent addition to our volunteer staff this year. She's doing the best she can given the resources we have, but she's making it work. Right, kids?"

Drake and Ava say cheerfully, "Right!"

Mr. Town smiles. "Good, good, good. Anything that keeps these little rascals off them dang computer games and learning something worthwhile is all right with me."

"Granddad!" Ava says, giving him a look. "Miss Lotus, we have to go. Thank you!"

It's comical, the way she's literally pushing him toward the door. His laugh is kind as he rolls his eyes at his granddaughter.

He looks at me and says, "Well, young lady, we won't keep you any longer. You and your friend keep on fighting the good fight. MacArthur Park schools always get the short end of the financial stick where Miami-Dade County is concerned. We have to stand up for our rights. So thank you for that."

"But . . ." I try to explain that he has it all wrong. I'm not fighting for the schools. I'm not fighting for the kids. I'm not fighting for anyone.

Not even myself.

But it's clear he's heard what he wanted to, and before I can change his mind, they're all gone.

Uncle comes back, poking his head in the door.

"They just wanted to meet you," he says. "Amya grew up in the community and used to come to the center, too."

"She looks young," I say, busying myself with stacking sheets of music I've copied from the internet for the kids.

"Yeah, she had Drake her senior year of high school. We went to school together. Amya is a nice girl, just . . . well, she didn't always make good choices. And she didn't have a knack for picking good men. But she is a great mom. A hard worker."

I turn and look at him. "Sounds like you like her, Unk!"

He grins. "No, no, no. Nothing like that. Amya was just always one of those girls I felt like I had to look out for. She was good people. Anyway, thanks for being here and chatting. The kids really are enjoying your class."

Most of the children have been picked up. We are moving room to room shutting off lights and making sure they are empty of kids.

We are both heading for the door when I ask, "Unk, have you ever heard of somebody called Buckwheat?"

He pulls a face. "Buckwheat? Chile, where in the world did you dig up that name?"

I shrug, unable to meet his eyes. "I just saw a meme, that's all."

His expression turns stony and his eyes hard.

"Yeah, I know who Buckwheat is. Another one of a long line of derogatory images American society embraced to dehumanize Black people." He sounds bitter.

"Was it really from a TV show?" I ask.

"It started as a series of short films as far back as the early '20s. Have you seen any of them on TV?" When I shake my head, he continues:

"Believe it or not, the *Our Gang* shorts were considered socially groundbreaking because they featured Black and white kids, all poor, all being, I guess, socially equal. At least, that's how some critics viewed it. But with today's lens, it's a humiliating look into the stereotypes that have plagued our people for centuries. What's got you thinking about all this?"

We're outside now, heading toward his car. He offers me a ride, but I tell him I'll walk. I say, "Just curious," because that's all I can manage. My throat feels thick, and my breathing is shallow.

I picture the meme again. My stomach is hot, and I feel my jaw tighten. My heart is racing, and the walk, the ocean air, the warmth of the afternoon sun—none of it is helping.

It's a feeling I'm not familiar with. Not really comfortable with. But it's here, just the same.

Anger.

I am really, really mad.

And I don't like it.

Not

    at

      all.

❧

For the rest of the week, we had after-school rehearsal.

Pure and utter madness.

The open house is all about staging. Rather than being in the PAC on a stage, we're going to perform in the atrium. The chorus will be on the stairs. Ensemble groups will be set up in different areas.

We'll be like a roving band of troubadours—medieval musicians—going from one area to the next depending on which song we are performing.

Our arrangement includes a few Broadway pieces, as well as ballet, jazz, and—the grand finale—an uptempo modern song. That part is cool.

The dance department is part of the performance, too, and all the musical disciplines are providing their music. Need to showcase all aspects of the school's arts program!

You would think musicians and dancers work well together, but you'd be sooooo wrong. Turns out, artists—musical, visual, dance—don't play well with others. *Sigh*!

It's Thursday evening. The performance is the next Tuesday. So. Much. To. Do.

We are all in the front hall atrium. There is a second atrium opposite the lunchroom café. Wind howls beyond the overhead glass dome. Thunder rattles above us. Lightning rips the sky with slashes of light pulsing like soundwaves. Maestro has a scowl to match the storm above. He isn't a patient man.

"We are not here to socialize. We are here to perfect our work," he says, softly but firmly. Maybe some of the kids from beginners' orchestra or dance think he isn't too mad since he isn't shouting.

Those of us in advanced orchestra know better. He raises his voice when he gets annoyed. But the more angry he becomes, the lower his voice gets.

Now, its tone is a baritone F4. Low and full of weight and gravel. He is working hard to keep his anger in check. He's not mad—he's seething.

I glance around, trying to use telepathy to warn the others to get it together. A few ill-timed horns blurt from the staircase. The rest of our orchestra remains silent. Soon, the others get smart and shut down the noise.

"Maestro is wound really tight," Tatiana whispers.

"I know, right?" I answer.

We spend the next hour repeating the same number over and over. It is Igor Stravinsky: *Finale* from Firebird. Not an easy piece, believe me. But beautiful.

"Musicians, this is an iconic ballet, and the music is very emotional. The tempo can change as quickly as love itself," Maestro says. A few kids snicker, but most maintain focus.

Eight ballerinas, girls I've never met before, drop onto the chilly concrete floor of the open space. I know how they feel. My fingers are cramping, and my neck aches.

Tatiana and I move among the violins in our section, making sure they are producing a high-quality sound from their instruments.

The horn section has returned from their position on the stairs to sit in the makeshift performance area.

By the time practice ends, I'm exhausted. My shoulders ache. My fingers feel like how Granny's must feel when she complains about her arthritis.

"I think everyone is doing well," Tati says. "It'll be fine. Don't stress so much." She gives me a pat on the back.

Me, stressed.

That is *so* not who I am.

But it's true. I am feeling *too* stressed. I didn't know how to handle it. As I turn to follow everyone else back to the orchestra room to gather our things to leave, I look up and find Adolpho looking at me. His jaw clenched tight.

I try not to let it bother me, the way he looks like he wants to squash me, but I can't help it. The hateful meme pops back into my head. When I meet his eyes a second time, I see the sneer. Cold and mean.

And I get a burning feeling deep in my belly.

❧

Tuesday, October fourth, comes fast.

The night before open house, instead of sweating over my

two solos—one with the full orchestra and one with a string ensemble—I pour all my energy into my hair. A clarifying wash to remove all the old gunk, then a deep conditioning, followed by gently detangling, separating it into sections, and finally loosely twisting it and wearing a satin sleep cap to bed.

As I'm drifting off to sleep, I picture what Rebel's face would look like if I were to tell her about the Adolpho situation. Her head might explode.

When I was little, Mom and Dad fought—a lot. Nothing physical. But they argued all the time. Then Granny would come over, and there would be more arguments. See, for me, conflict is scary.

Mom would cry, which made me cry. Then my dad would yell at her for "acting like a big baby," and Mom would yell at him for "acting like a big bully," and the whole cycle would start all over again.

I remember pressing myself against the floor beneath my bed one time. The memory makes me shudder. I must've fallen asleep under there that day. When I woke up, it was dark. And when I went to their bedroom, it was empty.

For a horrible few minutes, I was sure they'd both left. The memory haunts me. Much as I love my dad and love Mom, I'm glad they are no longer together. Now I have two separate parents who are good people, instead of married parents who were a lousy couple!

I take a few calming breaths and remind myself I am determined to feel beautiful, powerful, and strong.

I am nobody's Buckwheat!

But when I think about fighting back against Adolpho, making a stink, I feel cold inside.

It'll all work out. I have to believe that. It will all be okay.

⚜

The day of the show, I get a case of nerves. Butterflies jitterbug in the pit of my stomach.

Breathe, Lotus, breathe!

The night starts out strong. Mom, Granny, and even Derrick, the sometime-boyfriend, come to see me play. When the show begins, I walk through the orchestra to get everyone tuned.

The dancers look weightless as they float across the floor. It is a beautiful sight, with the lights and fog adding to their floaty appearance.

The show opens with my Bach Double with Maestro. Just like before, my nerves threaten to claw through my chest. I try not to make eye contact with Mama. Having her here is making me extra nervous.

Dad's voice whispers in my head. We did a FaceTime call earlier. He said he loved me and knew I was prepared and ready to impress. I cross my toes, hoping he was right.

Maestro leads me through the Bach Double, same as he did in our orchestra room. The effect of us playing back and forth, each following up the other's notes, is electrifying.

The applause is thunderous. Maestro clasps my hand,

and we take a bow; his grip is warm and strong. I'm sweating.

After that, I find myself enjoying and appreciating so many others' performances. The percussion ensemble, the guitars, and the dancers.

After my big part is done, I'm even part of an ensemble that plays a small set in the art room for the visual artists. Dion gives me a grin as he stands peacock proud in front of some of his work. My tongue practically hits the floor when I spot one of his creations.

"Dion!" I gasp. "That's . . . that's . . ."

"It's you, honey. You and all that fabulous hair!"

It's like one of the sketches he'd done during our first week of school when we were sitting together in the performing arts center. Only it's on a huge canvas. It's weird how he captures not only my face but my mood. He even enhanced the flower in my hair, painting it a bright orange and yellow. I'd never worn one that color, but now I want to.

"I can't believe you did this," I say.

A woman, no doubt a parent of someone in here, moves over to us. "That's you, isn't it?" she asks, looking between me and the painting. I nod. She continues, "I love it. The painting, and the hair!"

I give Dion a hug. "That is so beautiful, Dion. Thank you!"

"No, honey. Thank you! It's hard to find a muse. Just

keep doing what you're doing." He smiles. "Just keep on doing you!"

If I thought the night's biggest and best moment was finding a four-foot canvas with my face on it, I'd be wrong.

The highlight comes when, at the end of the evening, Maestro calls me and Tati to come stand with him on the platform.

"Parents, teachers, administrators, I want to take this opportunity to introduce my concertmaster and first chair, Lotus Bloom, and her second, Tatiana Lee," he says.

I feel that little shiver of joy and terror nibble at me.

Then comes a roar of applause. Am I shallow to admit how much that applause soothed my soul? I feel its warmth down to my toes.

He continues, "Miss Lee is an eighth grader who began study of the violin at age five. She is a gifted and talented young lady with a sophisticated work ethic."

I look at Tati, and her cheeks pinken as she bites her lip. She slides her hand over and hooks her little finger around mine. I give it a gentle squeeze, my heart hammering.

"And Miss Lotus Bloom, our concertmaster, is only a seventh grader. She earned this distinction by being one of the most truly gifted young musicians I've ever met. Her sense of timing and musicality are special and rare. Please join me in giving both these young ladies a round of applause."

I could have floated to the moon—and beyond! By the time it's over, I feel like my old self.

Too bad "feel" doesn't last.

In the music locker room, I see Adolpho and some other ninth-grade boys. I am still floating on a cloud and not paying much attention to them. Mom, Granny, and Derrick are waiting, and we're going out to celebrate.

As I unlock the locker, Adolpho blares, "Here she is! The queen of orchestra, herself! Meet . . . *Buckwheat, oh tay!*"

And just like that, all the applause, the praise, the memory of Dion's wonderful painting, all of it evaporates. I get a chill that turns into a shiver.

All of them are laughing. I feel sick. My face feels hot, and a nasty taste coats my tongue, my teeth, even my lips.

I want desperately to have a comeback. Some verbal weapon that would put him—all of them—in check.

But I am not that girl. I'm not the girl who comes ready to fight, to stand up. With the lump rising in my throat, I desperately wish Rebel was here. She'd rip Adolpho to shreds without breaking a sweat.

I want that to be the worst of it, but it isn't. Not by a long shot.

A boy I don't recognize throws a paper airplane into my hair. This causes a roar of laughter.

Then Adolpho says, "Snowball fight!"

They all begin blasting me with paper wads.

About five boys, all older and bigger, are pelting me with

116

wads of paper. Airplanes and little paper footballs, snow-balls, anything they can get their hands on.

The woolly mammoth is no match for such a battle.

I keep saying, "Stop! That's enough! Not funny!"

But they keep on pelting me. Their faces are red and full of . . . what? Anger? Aggression? Whatever it is, it's all directed at me.

I am scared, but too scared to cry.

Grabbing my violin and my music bag, I run out. The humiliation burns my face, my stomach, my soul. I shake my head until all the aircraft crash-land to the ground.

The ride to the restaurant is quiet, at least for me. Mom stops chitchatting with Granny and says, "Lotus, you're unusually quiet. You okay?"

A fat tear slides down my cheek, but I keep my face pressed against the glass. Granny, sitting with me in the back seat, turns to look at me.

"What's wrong with you, girl? Didn't like all that applause?" The urge to shove the tip of a paper airplane dead center into her press and curl is strong enough to make me bend over. "You're not going to throw up, are you?"

I can't look at Granny. Weakly, I mumble, "No."

I want to tell them what happened. Want to say, "A bunch of boys pelted me with wads of paper that might as well have been stones."

Want to say I'd gotten compared to a meme about a boy

named Buckwheat who looks like the enslaved people in Mr. Burke's history books.

I want to say a lot of things, but before anything comes out, Mom asks, "Was that boy there tonight? The one who has a crush on you. Adolpho, I think you said his name was? Mr. Paper Airplane."

My face presses harder against the cool glass of the car window. Hard enough to hurt. I can't look at either of them. I don't even want to go to the restaurant. I don't want to eat. I just want to go home.

"He was there," I answer in a voice so small and hurt I don't recognize it. "I'm fine, just really tired. Can we please go home?"

Mom and Granny exchange a look, and Mom says, "I remember those days. Puberty is an emotional time. We can go home. We'll celebrate some other time."

Granny lets out one of her snorts and says, "God knows your mama don't need the calories."

"Mama! I deserve to eat, too!" Mom snaps.

"I like a woman with a little meat on her bones," Derrick says.

"That's hardly an endorsement for being fat," Granny says dryly.

"Aww, Mama, she's fine just the way she is. Nowadays, they're called curvy girls," Derrick pipes in.

Is it wrong that I am praying for an animal to step into the road and send our car swerving away from the critter and into the ocean nine blocks away? I feel like my insides are coming undone, and the people I should be able to count on are—what was that vocab word? Oblivious. They haven't got a clue.

Mom looks at me, waiting for me to step in and smooth things over, as usual. I play oblivious, too.

I'm done.

Screw that!

For once, I don't have the energy or desire to fight her battle.

For once, I'm starting to think it's time to stand up and fight my own!

12

When you fall asleep with your mouth full of unspoken bitterness, it's hard to get rid of it the next morning, even with toothpaste.

I wake up Wednesday morning with a monster headache. No doubt stressed out because of what happened last night. I do a few aggressive rounds of yoga, stretch my body and my mind, and make a decision:

I am going to talk to the dean of students, Mr. Mackie, dean in charge of the seventh grade.

Calmly and maturely, I will tell him what has been happening and let him know I am not comfortable being treated like that. No hysterics. No drama. Just the facts, sir.

Ten minutes before the first bell, Mr. Mackie ushers me into his office. "Good morning, Miss Bloom, good to see you. Come in," he says. "What a great performance you gave yesterday. The maestro thinks very highly of you!"

He is a tall man with hooded eyes that make him look like he is keeping lots of secrets. Why not? Every other grown-up in my life is keeping some kind of secret.

The office is smaller than I thought it would be. And a little shabby. Also not what I'd expected. His window is small, his bookshelves old, and the carpet looks left over from some other school, same as the guidance counselors' offices at MacArthur.

"Please have a seat," he says, and I slide onto an itchy wool-covered chair. If his office was a song, it would be filled with deep bassoons and horns with mournful low notes. "Now, what can I help you with?"

This is it! The moment I push forward and try to take control of what's happening to me.

"Mr. Mackie," I begin, heart like a trumpet, notes rising higher and higher. "I've been experiencing some . . . uh . . . bullying. Here. At school. And, well . . . I need it to stop. It's . . ." My voice breaks and I suck in air. "It's really starting to affect me."

He leans forward, his bony elbows folding like the scrawny wings of a large bird. Fingers laced and unlaced on his hands as his whole body leans into the desk, his eyes intense.

"I'm so sorry to hear that," he says, sounding like he means it. He passes me a tissue the same automatic way you say "god bless you" when someone sneezes.

But his eyes never leave my face. They are deep

brown and searching. Like he is looking for some kind of answer.

I dab at my eyes, although I am sure I am not crying.

"I'm having trouble in main orchestra. As you know, Maestro chose me as first-chair violin and concertmaster. But Adolpho Cortez thinks he should be concertmaster. So now he and his friends keep bombing my head with paper balls and paper airplanes!"

I blow out a long breath, glad to get that off my chest.

Mr. Mackie sits back in his chair. The squeak of the hinges goes on so long it's like an echo. His thick brows draw together, and clouds form behind his rich brown irises.

"Adolpho Cortez?" he says.

"Yes." I nod. "He did not take it well, being replaced by me. I mean, I understand. Nobody likes being told someone is better. Especially someone younger. But I didn't ask for it. Had no idea Maestro was even going to do it. So, anyway, I was wondering if you could talk to him. Ask him and his friends to knock it off. I'm not trying to get anyone in trouble, but it's not fun. At all."

There! I'd gotten it all out. I blow out another long breath.

"Is . . ."—his voice falters—"is Maestro aware of the situation?"

I frown. I hadn't told Maestro.

"No," I say, "I thought I should come to you first." I had been sort of afraid that if I told Maestro, it might be worse for Adolpho.

"Good," Mr. Mackie said. "I will take care of the situation. We take bullying very seriously, Miss Bloom. I promise I'll take care of it!"

I leave his office feeling better. He'll handle it. Problem solved.

❧

In orchestra, Maestro assigns us new music to learn for the holiday showcase. Tatiana and I work with the first-section violins. Every once in a while, I feel Adolpho's glare scraping my back or glimpse his superior smirk.

He is being a total dragon. I ignore him, still feeling stronger now that I've taken a stand.

Working with the violins is fun. Orchestra types are different. Myself included. We don't think like other people, like other students. But mostly we understand one another. Despite all the goofiness, we get our group to settle down enough to practice our first piece for the concert. We finish and share a big, fat sigh.

Before we can say anything, Maestro speaks up.

"By the way, musicians," he says, "I am chairing the foundation that handles the International Youth Orchestra concert. This year's performance is in Paris the week after Christmas. They want candidates from each section—winds, percussion, and strings. I encourage those of you who are excelling in these areas to see me after the class about this opportunity."

My jaw hits the floor.

I'm going to Paris!

Now I have a chance. A real chance. Mozart plays in my chest. Class ends without any forced landings in my head. I go down front to Maestro's desk and hover while he speaks to a few other students. When it is my turn, I can barely hold myself together. I blurt:

"I want to go!"

His eyebrows, which at this point have taken on a life and language of their own during class, rise with a knowing tilt.

"Is that right?" he says.

"That's right," I answer. "My dad lives in Paris and works for an orchestra there. It would be amazing to go and participate with an orchestra of musicians from all over the world!"

I recognize my tone is too loud and sharp, bordering on desperate.

"Indeed, Miss Bloom. I shall have the appropriate paperwork here for you tomorrow. Your parents, or primary guardian, will need to sign the papers. You must have them back to me by October tenth. Good day," he says, turning to his next student.

The idea of being part of an international youth orchestra has me feeling giddy all day. Even when a paper airplane lands on the floor beside me in the hallway, missing my head, I don't freak. Mr. Mackie will handle the situation. I have faith.

I arrive at the café later than usual.

I'd been texting with Rebel, telling her my news. When I enter the café, I find Mercedes and the rest of our crew hunched over the lunch table staring at her phone.

"Can I see, too?" I ask.

They all sort of jump and look at me funny. Instantly, I know something's up. "What?"

YaYa, her ever-present lollipop pressed to her lips—today's flavor being orange—says, "Might as well show her." And Mercedes holds up her phone.

Someone filmed the paper ball attack in the music room and added a tagline, "Buckwheat be like . . . *it mus' be snowing on da' inside. Oh tay!*"

I feel the color drain out of my body.

It makes me want to throw up. My hands shake. I feel weak and drop into a chair. Taj gives me a look. "Take a deep breath. You could report it. I mean, if it's really bothering you."

If it's bothering me?

Seeing that image again leaves my hands and stomach feeling slippery. Mercedes's eyes glimmer from being the star of this little dramedy. When she grins, she reminds me of a shark. I suddenly feel like a clueless guppy.

She says gleefully, "Adolpho must secretly want your body, mi'ja. That's why he can't stop picking at you." Before she'd been all "burn him at the stake! Light the torches."

Now she is sounding like my mother.

I can't help glancing at Fabiola, alone at a corner table. She is staring right back. Her words replay in my brain, what she'd said about Mercedes:

I've known her a while.

She is a backstabber.

And the minute she can, she will turn on you.

I sit down and try to laugh it off. Try to eat, but everything tastes like dust.

Nothing is funny.

Can't they see that?

❧

Monday, Maestro calls me down front soon as I walk in.

"Miss Bloom, might I see you, por favor," Maestro calls out in his melodious tenor. A few kids glance my way with questioning looks. I set down my violin and glance at Tati.

I whisper, "Do you know what this is about?" My book bag drops onto my chair. She shakes her head.

"Miss Bloom?" Maestro is not known for his patience.

"Coming, uh, sir," I say. I always feel like I should call him Your Highness.

Maestro lifts an envelope as soon as I reach him. He says, "Here," handing it to me. "The application for the International Youth Orchestra. I have selected you as our candidate for their violin section. There is a form that I've already filled out and signed with my recommendation. There is another that you and your parents must sign. That form also lists the cost of the trip, which is sixteen hundred dollars. That includes airfare, lodging, and meals for the week."

He must've noticed how my eyes bugged out when he mentioned the price. Getting into the spot, going to visit Dad in Paris, would be a dream come true. And more than that, using that experience on my application would give me a huge boost in earning a scholarship to that pricey Parisian school. I'd be able to move and live there—permanently.

But that's a *ton* of money.

Maestro adds, his smooth Cuban accent playing piano notes over my senses, "Do not fear the cost. We were able to secure a thousand-dollar scholarship for each student selected for this program. However, your family will be responsible for the rest. And there is another form that asks you to submit a video of yourself playing. Can you manage that?"

I nod. "Yes, sir, I can do that."

"Good," he says. "Lotus Bloom, I am putting my faith in you that you will present yourself and conduct yourself with the grace and expertise you have shown me. Do you feel able and ready for this challenge?"

My mouth drops open. I say, "Yes, yes, I do!"

"Good, good! Now, let us move ahead and not focus on any petty squabbles with classmates. Concentrate on your art, your music. Lead with conviction and keep pushing yourself to do better than you did the day before. I would hate to see a talent as precious as yours squandered. Understood?"

I don't understand anything except that he is giving me his unconditional stamp of approval for the trip to Paris. I can't wait to call my dad. He'll flip!

I want to hug Maestro and squeeze his very serious face. I do not squeeze his very serious face, though, because that would be wrong. Instead, I say, "Thank you so much. I won't let you down!"

When I tell Tati and Anabel, Tati says, "Well, duh? Who else would get his endorsement? You're a natural."

"Hope my folks think so, too. Even though school is giving me a thousand dollars, I will still need six hundred dollars. I've only got about three hundred saved."

"You'll work it out," Anabel said.

The morning goes by with no incidents. No paper intruders. No memes. As soon as I get a free moment before lunch, I shoot a text to Rebel:

Whoop! Whoop! Maestro is recommending me for
Intl Youth Orchestra

Her response comes quick:

So happy for you! Let's get together tomorrow

Inside the cafeteria, I don't see Fabiola, so I return to my usual table. The approving words of Maestro are so uplifting, I figure even this group will celebrate along with me.

Wrong.

"So Maestro picked you for the Paris orchestra?" asks YaYa. "Congratulations!" I lean into her hug. YaYa is a big hugger.

I scoop a spoonful of chicken noodle soup into my mouth. Make *woo-woo-woo* sounds because it is very hot.

"Yes, he did. It's in Paris, but I think kids come from all over the world."

"Does Adolpho know?" Mercedes asks. This time the gleam in her eyes is unmistakable. So is the semi-sneer on her lips. I sit up from my soup.

"I'm not sure what Adolpho knows. I'm not even sure he wanted that spot," I say, because honestly I don't know.

"Well, let's ask him," she says.

Before I can even understand what is happening, Mercedes is up, yelling, "Adolpho! Adolpho! Hey, come here!" Me and YaYa and Taj all exchange questioning looks. Is she for real right now?

When Mercedes melts into her seat, the smirk evaporates into a total look of innocence. Adolpho comes over and makes a point of saying "hey" to everybody but me. *Ooo, I'm devastated.* Then Mercedes tells him:

"Your maestro has offered Lotus the violin spot on the International Youth Orchestra." Her tone is filled with glee. Why, she is practically floating on a cloud of good cheer.

Adolpho's head snaps around. He stares at me like he wants to choke me. His cheeks flush bright pink, and his floppy brown hair is wild on his shoulders. When he turns back to Mercedes, anger is vibrating off his body.

"We'll see about that!" When he leaves, I look at my so-called friend, Mercedes.

"What was that about?" I ask.

She shrugs, her smirk trying gamely for innocence. "I happen to know his parents have been pushing him to earn that spot since he was in seventh grade. He's been planning on it since last year," she says.

Wow! Passive aggressiveness as an art form. Is she a student of the art or a full-fledged professor?

Despite the overload of girl snark, I am determined to maintain my cool. And the confidence that has been building since Maestro talked to me that morning.

I am going to Paris—and I will represent Atlantis.

Dad and Maestro, even Mom, will be proud!

Part of me does feel a little guilty. Maybe Adolpho deserves to go, too. Then I think about how horrible he and his friends have been.

Sometimes it's exhausting trying to make everyone happy.

When will it be my turn? To be happy. To be proud—of *me*?

❧

I need a break from my so-called friends, so when I bump into Fabiola in the lunch line the next day, I ask, "Why

130

do you always sit alone? Do you not *want* to sit with anyone?"

Shoulder shrug. "I'd welcome company, I just don't seek it out. I am not a good fit into the different groups in here," she says, looking around. Another shrug, a toss of her waist-length braids.

"I like your flower," she says. I touch it gingerly. I feel naked without my flower.

Mercedes is watching and starts to frantically wave me over.

"Be right back," I say.

"What are you doing with *her*?" Mercedes asks with an epic eyebrow arch. She uses that thing like a sword.

I say I'm trying to meet more people. "She's nice, so why not?" I add a not-quite-authentic smile of positivity.

What I should say is *mind your own business*. What I really should say is *I'm tired of your not-quite-believable sweet act*. I am beginning to realize that Mercedes is toxic and bad for my chi.

"Awww," says YaYa, exaggerating her pouty face, "don't go!"

"You should come meet her, too," I say to YaYa, casual as I can. I see her pull her head back like a turtle. I see something like fear flit across her huge eyes. I sigh. "I'll see you guys later," I say, turning to walk away.

"I didn't know you were into girls," Mercedes says, matching her casual tone with mine. "Fabiola is a total lez."

"Girl, what is your deal!" says YaYa. "You don't seem to have a problem with Dion or any other gay male. So what if Fabi is gay? I'm not obsessed with getting all up in her business like you are!"

"I'm not obsessed with her, chica. Chill out, Ya. Do you, you know, need a Midol?" When Mercedes laughs at her own joke, her voice sounds hollow.

I hadn't been able to shake the image of Mercedes hunched over her phone, gleefully sharing the Buckwheat meme. I had begun to feel that YaYa was under Mercedes's spell.

If that was the case, however, the spell has been broken.

YaYa stands and says, "I think I will join you, Lotus."

We walk away, and I'm overcome with a feeling of love and good vibes. YaYa seems to be almost shaking. I know how hard that had to be.

"May we join you?" I ask Fabiola. YaYa doesn't speak, just nods her head, opening her eyes even wider than normal.

"Of course," Fabiola says.

Fabiola's hair is piled on her head and held in place with a beautiful scarf. It's a perfect pineapple—that's what you call that style. Her stiff politeness soon melts away, and the three of us get along really well.

"Can I sketch your face?" she asks me.

I almost spit out my pomegranate juice (Pom, my favorite),

covering my mouth with my fingers and getting dribbled with the purpley-red drink.

"Omigod! Am I just funny looking or what?" I'm laughing, which draws a wide, warm smile from her.

"It's the angles of your face," she says. When she reaches over to trace the line from my ear to my chin, I swear I hear Mercedes cackle.

"Did she tell you that I was 'a lez'?" she asks, smiling.

YaYa sputters, "She's . . . she's just rude like that. It's nobody's business!" Her normally golden cheeks flame hot pink.

Glancing over my shoulder until I make eye contact with Mercedes, I shrug. "Be my guest. I was so honored and amazed when my friend Dion displayed a portrait of me at open house." I pause, realizing something:

"I didn't see you that night."

She is already sketching in the sketchbook. Her eyes are down, voice steady.

"My mother was having surgery. She is very ill." She says it so simply, so matter-of-fact, I blink a few times, unsure I'd heard her right.

"Is she okay?" I ask.

Fabiola shrugs. "No, not really. Now, lift your chin a little," she directs, pausing to take a dainty bite of her sandwich before continuing to scratch lines and curves onto the page. When she looks up, she adds, "It has been an ongoing problem. Maman is strong. I have faith."

When she drops her eyes, it's clear art is her safe space, so I let her have it.

YaYa and I exchange looks again. There is something so bone-deep cool about this girl. It's like being over here with Fabi automatically chills me out and slows me down.

After that day, me, YaYa, and Fabiola have formed our own lunch group.

Instead of being stuck inside, we are eating in the courtyard at black wrought-iron tables. We meet outside beneath a labyrinth of palm tree shadows crisscrossing the walkways. It's beautiful and I want to relax, but I find my mind jumps uncomfortably several times to the weedy courtyard with its cracked concrete and unexplainable smells back at MacArthur.

Dion, Taj, and this other dude from visual arts, Benz, have joined our café table, too. It's been three days since I first ditched Mercedes, taking a break from her drama.

Fabiola takes out her sketchbook. She's turning in her drawing of me for an assignment due next hour.

"Yes, honey, yes!" says Dion with all the subtlety of psychedelic thigh boots. "You've got those cheekbones, and when the light kisses your dark skin, it's a glow up from the flo' up!"

"And all the planes and shadows of your face are illuminated," adds Fabiola. She is tilting her head, regarding me like a sculpture. I become a little self-conscious.

Then when I catch Taj staring at me, too, I dip my head

and tell myself to stop being weird. Too late. I'm feeling tingly, and my face is hot—not sun hot, either.

"Stop moving!" commands Fabiola. "I'm almost finished."

I shift my eyes to Taj. (I am allowed to turn my head. The artist says so.) I say, "I didn't know so much was going on with my face."

He smiles and says softly, "It's a very nice face." Then he reaches out and gently touches my hair.

"It's so pretty. It's so you." He says it so quietly, I think I imagined it.

"*OOOOOO, weeee!*" Dion sings out, and instantly I know I was not imagining anything. "*Hon-eyeeee,* love is in the *air!*"

It is *so* embarrassing, but D's over-the-top-ness makes everyone laugh, and only the people at our table know he's talking about me and Taj, so it's okay. The awful knot of tension that had been gripping my heart releases. I feel light as the wondrous notes of Mozart's Concerto no. 5 in A Major, floating like the ballerinas from the open house show.

The feelings inside me become a beautiful web of long violin notes singing in the tater tot–scented air of the café. I am lost in the lovely world of notes and sound.

Until, heading back inside to place my tray on a rolling rack, I walk right into Adolpho.

He looks over his shoulder, his expression saying, "All

good." But when he sees it's me, an ugly snarl claims his whole face.

Anger boils off him, and he seems unable to speak. Strangled words squeeze out of him, and his lips twist into a nasty grin.

"You're not getting that seat in the international orchestra. That's my seat. *My* opportunity!"

Venom, ripe and curdling. Thanos in *Avengers: Endgame*.

Now it's me who's lost her voice. But this time, I can't stay quiet. It takes a second, but I say, "That's between you and Maestro. I didn't even know about your plans for Paris, or any of that. He said he was happy to recommend me."

He turns all the way around. Kids are streaming past us. He shakes his head slowly, like he's trying to explain Shakespeare to an idiot.

"Uh-un. You don't get it. You're in trouble now. You're a puny SEVENTH GRADER, and you need to stay in your lane!"

He storms away.

Cymbals clatter in my head.

What on earth is he talking about? Why would I be in trouble? I think about my talk with Mr. Mackie. Everything had been fine. It had been a week, and, other than some dirty looks, I hadn't had much contact with Adolpho . . . I figured Mr. Mackie had handled it and everything was settled.

So, what did he mean?

Even though I know I did nothing wrong, dread follows me around for the rest of the day. What is Adolpho planning?

✿

When I get home, Mom is still at work. So is Derrick. They usually come home together, anyway. I'm glad for the quiet. A chance to think and practice my music without a bunch of small talk that feels like it's getting smaller all the time.

I'm heading down the hall toward my room, shuffling the mail I snagged from the community boxes. I keep the key because mail retrieval falls under the heading of "Lotus Bloom's official household chores."

That's when I spot it—a letter addressed to Mom and Daddy from Mr. Mackie. I don't care one bit about Federal regulations about only opening mail that's addressed to you, so I open it:

Dear Mr. and Mrs. Bloom,

This letter is to inform you that we have scheduled a conference regarding your daughter, Lotus Bloom, due to severe dress code violation based on the unruly nature of her hair. If she does not adjust her appearance and bring herself up to code by the date of the conference, on Wednesday, Oct. 12, she could be suspended from school indefinitely.

I have attached the current code of conduct here
for your reference.

Our student dress code is clear—students must
maintain a manner of dress and personal style
that does not disrupt or engage other students.
Lotus's unruly hair has created a disturbance in the
classroom and must be taken seriously.

If you have any questions prior to the deadline,
feel free to contact me at the school.

Sincerely,
Edgar J. Mackie, Dean of Seventh-Grade Students
Atlantis School for the Performing Arts

My hair created the disturbance? What?

Suddenly, I remember the conversation I had with
Maestro. What he'd said about me getting his recommendation for the International Youth Orchestra.

*". . . let us move ahead and not focus on any petty
squabbles with classmates. Concentrate on your art, your
music."*

Did that mean that I should ignore any ol' humiliating
thing that happened? That I should suffer for my art?

A tightness enters my chest and squeezes so hard I think
I'm breaking in two. I picture Adolpho's smug grin. Mercedes's smirk. The dean of students and his long, praying
mantis limbs.

And the uncomfortable feeling of anger is back, sur-rounding me like a cage.

I can't do this. I've been pushed and pushed and pushed. For the first time in my life, backing down is the last thing I want to do!

13

The letter upsets me so much that everything inside me goes silent.

I don't give it to Mom until dinnertime.

Our kitchen smells of pot roast. Normally, I love the smell. Rich brown gravy, onions, carrots. But today I have no appetite.

"Why're you so quiet?" Mom asks. "This is your favorite." She chops lettuce and cucumbers for salads.

I give her the letter. What I want is for her to become outraged. I want her to declare, "Yes, by god! We will fight this to the bitter end!" I really need her on my side. Or at least to help me understand how to fix this.

None of that happens, especially after I tell her I think Adolpho has something to do with it. Instead, Mom flips the freak out! Like, ballistic!

She starts in on me, letting me know she is *not* on my side:

"I told you not to make waves, Lotus!" and "I told you this boy probably has a crush on you." And, "I told you to just ignore it. You didn't. Now you could be kicked out of this school." And her favorite, "How is this going to look on your record, getting kicked out of a prestigious school of the arts? Well, there goes your so-called music career!"

The tears well up, but I hold on to them. They are *my* tears, and I'm not about to share them with someone who won't even try to be on my side.

I draw a deep, shaky breath and try to defend myself, even though I'm not exactly great at confrontation.

"Mom, they want me to change my hair. My hair! That's not right. Can't you see that?" Even as I'm saying it, I hear the whine in my tone. I don't sound strong. Defiant. More like I'm begging to be heard.

And I hate how it sounds. Like off-key wind instruments struggling to compete with a bassoon.

"Your hair!" she says. She eyes my afro with contempt. "Everything is always about your hair, Lotus. There are more important things in the world. Besides, I wanted to do something about that woolly bush a long time ago. But *oh, no*! Your father made a big deal about how it was your self-expression. How it was your right. I'll bet he's loving this!"

The last thing I want is for her to know I haven't told Dad yet. Everything in me is squeezing. Especially my heart. No, I haven't told Dad. But he would stand by me and support me. I know he would.

The other letter, the recommendation from Maestro, has grown moist and wrinkly in my hand beneath the table. A knot the size of a Beethoven bust is lodged in my chest. Once I tell Dad about the recommendation, I'll also need to tell him about my application to the International School of the Arts in Paris.

Too many thoughts and feelings. My head begins to pound. Beautiful chunks of pot roast stir on my plate as I push them around with my fork in as aimless a pattern as I feel.

It doesn't take long before I can't bear sitting at the table with Mom and Derrick any longer, if she's just going to rehash my misery for dinnertime amusement. She doesn't try to stop me when I decide to eat in my room. But I'm a bit shocked when I look over and realize Derrick is giving Mom a funny look. He looks at me and offers a smile. When he looks back at Mom, he gives his head a tiny shake, then looks away.

Was that sympathy? Understanding? From Derrick? I know it's time to get out now and head to my room as fast as possible.

🪷

Posters and sheet music cover almost every inch of my walls.

My favorite quote, paired with a photo illustration of a gleaming violin, stares at me:

Music Is My Favorite Hiding Place.

Normally, that poster makes me feel warm. Makes me smile. Now all I can think about is this stupid letter and

Mom's reaction. And how I wish I could focus more on how to tell Dad how the International Youth Orchestra might be the recognition I need for a scholarship to the International School of the Arts.

The one he has no idea I've applied to, and no idea I'd forged his and Mom's signatures on to.

I have to think. *Think, think, think*!

My violin lies on my floral comforter. It feels familiar and graceful in my palms. I dust rosin on the bow, adjust the strings. Then I open my YouTube app to a song I've been practicing.

"Way Maker" is a beautiful piece. I put my violin up to my chin and play along. The song, I read once, was originally written as a worship song by a Nigerian artist. I've always liked that.

When I begin to play, I try to feel the beauty of the music. Try to see the colors and feel my soul transport to other times and places. I *need* to transport. But no matter how hard I press the violin beneath my chin, I can't pick up the vibe.

In the mirror, the reflection staring back is all wrong. My stance is all wrong. I am strangling my instrument, holding too tightly at the neck and moving in a herky-jerky motion.

Adolpho. I look like Adolpho when he plays.

I hit pause on YouTube.

What I need is to talk with Rebel. If anyone understands conflict, it's her.

I text:

Reb please check in.

Then I pace. I sit in a lotus pose, trying to find my chi. Hoping all this conflict hasn't permanently killed it.

Still, no answer from my friend. I send another text.

Don't make me beg. 9-1-1!

Several minutes pass. I feel so stressed that I am beginning to itch. I need a distraction. Clicking on the small television on my dresser, I see the news come on.

"Closer to home," the news lady is saying, "a tenacious group of students protest outside a special Thursday-night session of the Miami-Dade school board meeting . . ."

I scoot closer to the television. The lady behind the desk disappears, replaced by a young dude on NE Second Avenue. Behind him, students and grown-ups march, chanting:

"*Brown v. Board of Education* still applies. Black schools matter. Save our schools!"

And right there in front, as if I've summoned her with my thoughts, is my favorite woman on fire, Rebel Mitchell.

The young dude reporter begins interviewing Rebel. He asks, "What motivated you to organize this group and come here tonight?"

She says:

"MacArthur Park schools deserve to have working bathrooms, a cafeteria with ceilings that don't leak, and classrooms where you can concentrate on the teacher and not the cockroach sunning itself on the windowsill." She exhales, then straightens her shoulders and looks directly into the camera. "In the words of famous Black poet Audre Lorde, '*Your silence will not protect you.*' That's why we're speaking up!"

That poet she mentioned, Audre Lorde? I'd seen her poster in Rebel's room so many times. But I never paid attention to it.

I cringe. It feels like I've spent a lifetime not paying attention.

Instinctively, my gaze drifts to another poster quote hanging on the back side of my own door. It came from a Black woman who wrote this bestselling book, *You Are What You Tweet*. Her work popped up on my social media, and I enjoyed her positivity.

> Kindness is universal. Sometimes being kind allows others to see the goodness in humanity through you. Always be kinder than necessary.
>
> —GERMANY KENT

Is it time for kindness?
Or is it time to speak up—and fight back?

14

It's almost 11:30 when I finally hear from Rebel. She doesn't bother with a text.

"Girl, what is up? What's wrong?" she says when I pick up the phone.

"Well, first, let me congratulate you. I saw you on TV tonight—you looked great!" I say.

"Thanks! That's the reason I didn't see your texts right away; I got so many messages about tonight's protest. I'm sorry, Lo. What's up?"

All of a sudden, all the stress and butterflies of the past few days, weeks, bubble in my stomach. I feel my insides lurch. "Rebel, I'll call you back . . ."

Then I race from the room and into the bathroom, where bad things proceed. Very bad things.

When I finally get myself together, rinse my mouth, and stagger back to my bed, I realize I hadn't shut off my phone. Soon as I pick it up, I hear Rebel's voice.

"Are you okay? I know when you get stressed out you start hurling. Tell me right now"—her voice rises into the tone she saves for frightening salesgirls or snooty waitstaff—"what is going on with you?"

It takes a bit to get the words past my throat, which feels totally raw. A few deep breaths later, I rasp, "I'm in so much trouble, and I don't know what to do!" Okay, I admit, I may have gone a little heavy on the drama.

"Explain," she says. I can't look at her, but I can picture her, a small rectangle on my phone, sitting crisscross on her bed. Reading glasses tipped on her nose like somebody's grandma.

I explain.

Once I have the whole story out, I say, "It should have been my best day ever, yesterday, finding out I could win a seat to Paris, but instead . . ."

She cuts me off.

"Uh, hold up. Are you telling me a bunch of boys have been throwing paper airplanes at your head; *assaulting you*? And when you told on them, the school put *YOU* on notice? Is that what you're telling me?"

The burning and bubbling come back. My belly is under siege. I hadn't thought about how much Rebel scares me when she gets in attack mode. I remember why I didn't tell her before. Once I let her loose on this, she'd be full-tilt. What if she tries to make me do something I might not want to do?

"Well . . . ," I drag out, "I wouldn't call it an 'assault.'

147

I mean, it's just paper airplanes, but it's bothering me, that's all."

"Lo, it's *bothering* you? Really? That's all you've got to say about a group of entitled, jealous jerks pounding on you with paper weapons? And now the school is threatening to force you to cut *your* hair, change who *you* are, to suit them? Are you kidding me right now?" Rebel is breathing fire.

I don't know how to answer her or if I *should* answer her or if I should run away and never come back.

"Rebel, I just needed to talk to someone. I don't know what to do—about Mom, about the school, about anything. All I know is I don't want to cut my hair. And I don't want to lose my chance to get into the International Youth Orchestra."

I need Paris more than ever before.

The International Youth Orchestra. The scholarship. The new school.

A fresh start. A big, fat Do-Over!

She lets out a long, long sigh. If activism fails, she has a future as an acting coach. Girlfriend could give lessons!

"Does your dad know yet?"

"I . . . I haven't told him yet."

Doubt, scratchy as a wool blanket on the beach, rubs at my insides. I think I know what my dad will say. Surely, he'll be on my side, right? So what's holding me back?

My heart breaks into a marching rhythm as my brain

tries convincing itself that Dad will back me a hundred percent.

Rebel, unaware of my doubt, releases a long sigh. "Tell him, girl. Tell him as soon as possible. Then you have to make a plan and take a stand. I know how you hate to fight, but, girl, somebody has started a fight *with you*; now you need to finish it!"

The thought of conflict gives me hives.

I'm all about yoga and herbal tea; flowers behind my ear. I don't argue or make waves. I chill. Sure, Rebel makes fun of me for it, but I like how I am.

Rebel's insistence that I fight back leaves my hands clammy and my breath trapped in my lungs. I don't want to fight. I just want everybody else to realize they are wrong and do the right thing.

By four in the morning, I am tired of tossing and turning. I feel hot and sweaty. Tangled in bedsheets. My brain keeps bouncing from the sight of those boys' angry faces as they drilled me with paper planes, to the recommendation from Maestro, to the awful letter from Mr. Mackie, to my mom's rare tirade, and, finally, to Rebel's righteous indignation.

It just plays over and over on an endless loop.

What am I going to do?

By 4:15 a.m, I can't take it anymore. I call Dad. It's ten in the morning where he is. And I'm shocked when he answers sounding wide awake.

"Hey, ma chère, comment vas-tu?"

"Je ne vais pas bien, mon père." Yes, I have been practicing my French. Despite feeling so *ick*, a little tickle of pride wedges between the feelings of panic because I understood him and was able to answer. Progress, right?

Okay, no more stalling. Here's goes nothing!

"Well, I know something must be wrong for you to be calling me at four in the morning your time," he says.

Then he launches into a list of questions.

"Are you sick? Are you not well? Is there a problem with your mother?" I let him finish his string of questions, building up the strength to tell him. The mention of Mom reminds me of the covered bowl of stew by my bed. Even though she was upset with me, she'd brought it in with a small bottle of ginger ale. Taking care of me, like always.

He will be on my side. He will know what to do. He can help. That is what I tell myself.

"Dad, I need to talk to you," I say. I clear my throat. "I have a problem."

"What kind of problem?" he asks.

After several hard swallows, I draw a deep breath, exhale, and tell him everything. The whole story—well, almost the whole story, since I do not mention the application for a scholarship to an arts school in Paris. I'll save that for another time.

But I do tell him about being pelted with paper, about earning the recommendation and possibly coming to Paris the week after Christmas, and about the letter saying if I don't cut my hair, I'll be suspended.

"This whole thing has me trippin'. I don't know what to do." I can hear Daddy breathing and even the slow, deliberate rhythm of the air moving through his lungs feels judgy.

There is a pause. It gets longer . . . and longer. And . . . *longer.*

"Dad! Are you still there?"

"That's a lot of information. I do wish you'd let me in on all of this sooner," he says.

"Me too," I say in a small voice. A whisper.

"Lotus," he says, and hearing my name (instead of *ma chère* or *chérie*) lets me know he is serious. I feel my insides suck in as I wait. "The chance to audition for the International Youth Orchestra could be a once-in-a-lifetime opportunity. Baby, you've got to do whatever you can to make that happen."

"I know, but, Dad," I say, "they want me to cut my hair. You're not saying . . ."

"No! Definitely not. You don't need to cut your hair. But, baby girl, life is about compromise. Isn't there a compromise for you and your hair? Like, couldn't you wear it another way for a while? Until this drama settles down?"

"But you always said how much you loved my natural hair," I say, feeling exhausted and wrung out. "Why should I have to change?"

"You don't have to do anything. We always have a choice,

ma chère. We also have consequences. Do you want to risk yours?"

The silence bears down on me like a full-note rest. The absence of his full support crashes like a cymbal, shattering my resolve.

"Well," I begin, thinking of the possible consequences of fighting the school, "I guess not, not really. It's just, well, it's not fair." I'm sitting in the shadowy room. I haven't turned on the lights. My window is open, and somewhere in the distance a horn on a ship honks into the night.

"Life isn't always fair, Lotus. I've told you that. Sometimes success means sacrifice. Look, baby; finally, finally you're at a school where you can really learn something about music, about your craft. Isn't that what you've always wanted?" he asks.

"Yes, but . . ."

Dad rolls on, talking over me, not *hearing* me. I listen, feeling myself disappear into the shadows, as faint as a ghost note evaporating into dust.

"It's what I've always wanted for you, too. We both know how your mother feels. She couldn't care less if you ever took the stage in a grand hall. Or gained international acclaim," he says.

I flinch.

I picture him there, in Paris, living the perfect bachelor life, living his dream with his music, and a tinge of something stings me.

Mom is here. She makes sure I eat every day. She's the one who spoons leftover stew into a covered dish and sneaks it into my room. She's the one helping me detangle and maintain my hair, even though she wishes I would straighten it.

And she might not be a fan of my style or my choices, but at least she's here.

Dad is still talking. "I care. We care. You and I do. Just think about it. How can you give a *little*—just enough to get the other side off your back? I'm not telling you to do anything drastic like cut your hair or straighten it. But what about braids or some other natural hairstyle? Think about it, baby. Just think about it. This is what we've always dreamed about for you."

The more he talks, the farther away he seems.

When I hang up, I am more confused than ever.

Is compromise the answer? Or have both my parents abandoned me in my hour of need?

I return the phone to its charger and flop onto my back.

. . . *4:40* . . . *5:00* . . . *5:20* . . .

Sand burns in my sleepy eyes, but my mind won't stop churning.

What if I did wear my hair braided? I've never really liked having braids. They give me a headache.

But I've seen lots of girls with braids that were amazing. Fabiola's hair is amazing. But isn't it their choice? Why do I need to choose something just to make someone else feel better?

The alarm sounds at 6:15, approximately eight minutes after I finally fall asleep. I don't get up until Mom comes in at 7:20.

She immediately rushes over to the bed and puts the back of her hand on my forehead. Very Florence Nightingale. (By the way, Florence Nightingale—nurse, born in Florence, Italy. You're welcome.)

"Mom, I'm fine," I say, gently taking hold of her hand. Her skin is warm. She is dressed for work. Her own finely relaxed hair is bone straight and plastered into a compliant bun. She's like Corporate Mama Barbie—complete with neat blue suit, crisp white blouse, and sensible pumps.

We just stay like that for a moment—me feeling the warmth of her skin; her, with soft brown eyes, searching for the right thing to say.

I cave first.

"Mom, I'm sorry. I'm really, really sorry for . . . for . . . ," what? What am I sorry for? I don't even know anymore. I sit up so I can face her better, and all I know is I feel like I've caused trouble and ought to be sorry for something. "I'm just sorry for causing trouble. I just want those boys to stop hitting me with paper balls."

She grabs me into a great big ol' mama bear hug. "Boys can be stupid. That's a proven fact."

"I spoke with Dad, told him everything," I say. I can feel her stiffen, but I plow ahead. "He suggested a compromise. Maybe some other hairstyle."

"You mean like braids? Chile, I can't even picture you in braids. I haven't gotten your hair braided since you were six. And you did not like it," she reminds me.

I pull away from her and draw a deep breath.

"Mom, can I please stay home today? I'm exhausted. After everything that happened, I just need a little rest, then I'll work on my hair." I hadn't even twisted it last night in all the confusion. It's as tangled as my emotions.

I can see the inner struggle waging behind her eyes. Miss a day of school? On purpose? Blasphemy! However, she gives me one more hug and a peck on the forehead. Stands, straightening her work suit.

"Well, I expect to see a new you when I get home," she says. "Don't spend the whole day in here playing with that fiddle."

Fiddle. Like I'm in a fairy tale.

"Promise!" I say.

"And I'll help, with your hair, with whatever else. I love you, baby."

"Love you, too, Mom."

She leaves, but not before giving me a ton of instructions on locking the doors and staying safe. Somehow between her entering the room and leaving I've gone from twelve to preschool age.

Okay, so maybe I did cave—a little. I hate when we fight, even when I know I'm right. I didn't want to fight. Not with her. Not with anybody.

Maybe, just maybe, making this little change will calm the situation down and give me peace. Maybe there is another natural style that really works for me and doesn't make everybody else so uncomfortable.

It might not be so bad, giving myself an upgrade—not if it means getting along with everyone and still getting what I want most, right?

If I pull it off, maybe everyone will feel like I'm enough—good enough. Maybe I'll feel it, too.

15

On Monday, in piano lab, Mercedes has already moved to a new seat. I watch as her face darkens when I walk in.

She gives me an eye roll and says, "Your hair is *different*."

My hair *is* different.

I'd spent Friday and the rest of the weekend working out hairstyles. Conditioning, separating, scalp massaging, prepping and twisting my hair. Mom helped when she got home, and Derrick actually hung out with us. We watched a classic movie—*Imitation of Life*.

Mom had always told me that the movie was one of her favorites, but I'd never seen it. By the end, both of us were sobbing and even Derrick had a tear on his cheek. It's the story of this white woman single mom who befriends a Black woman. The white woman becomes famous; the Black woman becomes her live-in maid.

But the Black woman's daughter doesn't like being the

daughter of "the help." She's light enough to "pass," or pretend she's not Black. It breaks her mother's heart. In the end, when the Black mama dies, the girl, who has spent her life living a lie, is devastated.

Long after the movie ended and the lights were out, I lay in my bed thinking about the movie, hearing the soulful wail of gospel legend Mahalia Jackson singing the funeral song. And I wondered:

Am I about to do the same thing? Am I trying to live my life as somebody I don't want to be in order to escape who I am?

On Saturday, I went ahead with Project Compromise. I tried not to think of it as Project Sellout. Mom set up an appointment with a braid lady in our neighborhood.

It took her four hours to twist up all this hair. Not long, really, for braids. Twists were faster, and the size I'd chosen was on the bigger side.

Chunky twists now hung from the crown of my head to my bra line.

Mom had promised to take me out to eat. She and Derrick picked me up. When she saw me, she sprinkled praise like glitter upon me.

"You look great," she'd said. "I know it's not your beloved afro, but it's nice and neat and should keep you out of trouble."

Something about the way she glided over what I wanted, and whether or not it was worth fighting for, took a little more music out of my soul. And I felt naked without my trademark flower.

Shockingly, the increasingly involved Derrick gave his own head a shake.

"I don't think you should've changed it. I liked your afro. They're common now. Why, in this day and age, should you have to change?"

My mouth dropped open, but Mom's voice rode over anything I had to say. Her snapping at Derrick was almost as surprising as *him* standing up for me when neither of my own parents would.

The two of them sniped in their indirect, passive way as we ate Chinese. However, the power of carb coma soon took over. Only so much rice and noodles can you consume before your mind glazes over.

Of course, that was nothing compared to the beating I took from Rebel. She stopped by unexpectedly, and Mom let her in. One minute I was wearing earbuds and following the rhythm of a sweet piece of music. The next thing I knew— World War III.

"Girl, what have you done with your hair? What next? Please tell me you are not straightening it. Would you wear blue contacts just because everybody said so?"

She raged and raged. I wanted to stop her, but every time I opened my mouth, my lips trembled so bad I couldn't form words.

"Omigod, Lotus. Please, please, please learn to stand up

for yourself. You treated that afro like your precious pet. You loved it!"

"I might love it like this or in some other style, too. That's why you experiment." Okay, I knew how lame I sounded, but what else could I say?

"One reason I came over tonight was to tell you we've been talking to a local attorney, and she thinks we might have cause for a lawsuit. I wanted to ask you—once again—to come and stand with us, fight with us. But what was I thinking? You can't even fight for yourself!"

"That's not fair!" The words blurt out before I can think of anything else.

"Tough!" she snaps back. "Life's not fair!" So everyone keeps telling me.

One minute she was there, the next, exit stage right. The latest installment of the Rebel Show.

And—*scene*.

Rebel out!

She didn't catch my broken expression, a final act of despair to an audience of none. I was disappearing a little more each day. How long before I was completely gone?

❧

Maybe I could be thrilled with my new twists.

Still, it's hard to be thrilled when you are being forced to do something you don't want to.

I glance at Mercedes and her smirk. None of this is her

business. I'm more than a bit annoyed with her. Not enough to call her out, but still, I have other things on my mind.

"Yep!" I give her the same fakey-fake happy face I'd shown to Maestro. Then I look away, signaling I'm not all that interested in her reply. Still, as other kids stream into the room, they all have some comment about my hair.

"I like it!"

"The afro was better."

"Wish my hair was that long."

"This beats the afro."

"No, it doesn't."

"The afro was cool."

. . . and so on.

Eyes bulge when I walk into orchestra.

I move toward my seat, trying to look breezy and care-free, even though I'd spent more than an hour selecting today's wardrobe. Tight skinny jeans; an oversized, patchy bohemian blouse; tiny wedge sandals; and gold-rimmed, circular rose-colored glasses.

"Look at you!" Anabel says. "Your hair! You look so different."

Tati tilts her face up toward me.

"Wow! Nice hair. But hope you didn't do that just because the bozos were messing with you," Tati says with a grimace.

I feel my cheeks get warm and instantly shake my head. "No, no, no. Just wanted to try something new." Then I do this free-spirited curtsy and smiled my big happy, friendly, never-stressed smile.

Is she convinced?

Am I?

⚜

Class ends without another paper-ball assault. Maestro calls to me as everyone is leaving. My heart begins drumming double time. I can't help thinking about his "advice" about avoiding "petty squabbles."

Had he really thought that my being humiliated on a daily basis was a "petty squabble"?

I wonder how much he knew about my complaint to Mr. Mackie. I wonder if he *really* hadn't noticed those boys burying me under piles of notebook paper.

The adoration I'd had for him from the beginning was fading.

Still, I decide to do my best breezy-all-right-with-the-world performance. In A major. Adagio, even.

"Yes, sir!" I sing out.

"You were absent Friday?" He says it like a question even though we both know he already has the answer.

"Yes, sir!" I answer quickly, staring at him through my rosy vintage lenses.

"Were you ill or simply embarking on a makeover?" he asks.

His question sends a hot wave of anger through me. An emotion that I rarely acknowledge. Asking if I was *home "embarking" on a makeover.* Like he didn't understand why that would be necessary.

"No. Just didn't feel well. Didn't want to risk passing anything on if I was getting sick." I toss in a beefy ha ha ha. "Who knows when the next pandemic will strike."

"Yes, well, I do hope you are okay. Rehearsal is important. I'm sending emails to all the parents. You are to report after school every Tuesday and Thursday until the week before the holiday concert."

"I'll make sure and tell my mom to look for the email," I say, backing away before he can dismiss me.

❧

I'm glad for lunchtime. Talking about my hair was making me tired.

Wish that had been the end of it.

At the bistro table in the courtyard with Fabiola, Taj, and Dion, plus a few of Dion's friends, a tsunami of displeasure erupts.

"What did you *do*??" cries Dion with a stunned expression when he sees me. "Honey, I saw you earlier and figured you were new to the school. I didn't even realize it was you. What did you do to that glorious 'fro?"

Fabiola says, "Is this about Mr. Mackie and the pampered, overindulged Adolpho?" Her voice is much quieter than Dion's, but it holds power.

Then there's Taj, who says, "Um, no offense, but you just don't look like yourself."

Well! So much for getting off the subject.

After a few deep breaths, I smile gamely, trying for sincerity.

"Come on, you guys! I like it. Besides, it doesn't mean the 'fro is gone forever. I just wanted to try something new!"

Silence.

Eyes averted.

No one here is buying my act. After that, I struggle to get through lunch. Taj, Dion, and even Fabiola avoid making eye contact, only sneaking glances, even as we share small talk.

The whole episode leaves me feeling sad and alone.

❧

On Tuesday, I feel each second tick off the clock. It's the day before my big conference. In the morning, Mom is really pushing the fake cheer, telling me how proud she is of me, telling me how much I'll appreciate changing my hair "in the long run." What does that even mean?

"I am sorry about yesterday," Fabiola says at lunch. It's been raining on and off, so we are eating inside. "You seemed really sad when you were leaving. I did not mean to hurt your feelings. I'm sorry."

I let out a big sigh. Top it off with a heathy heap of shrugs.

"It's okay," I lie. "I mean, I didn't think it would be a big deal. I *am* just trying something new."

Today my hair is still in fat twists, only this time they're pushed back and held in place by a brightly colored head wrap serving as a wide headband. My maxi dress has the same magenta, brown, and pink swirls as the head wrap. And I've topped it off with gold-tinted sunglasses.

"You look very pretty today, as always," Fabiola says, French-Creole accent adding a half-note lilt to her words. We stand side by side at the pasta cart. I get my usual— butter noodle bow-tie pasta, covered in a mild butter sauce and topped with peas, carrots, and tiny florets of broccoli. Fabiola carefully places her plate of spaghetti on her tray, and we join the boys at our table.

"Hey, guys," I say, keeping my gaze from touching their eyes.

"Hey," Taj and Benz say back.

Dion is absent. I want to ask where he is, but the effort seems like more than I have to give.

After about five minutes of brutal awkwardness, Fabiola puts her fork down and turns to me.

"Lotus," she begins, "none of us want to hurt your feel-ings." Taj shakes his head until his long, dark curls swing. Even Benz agrees, though I am sure he has no idea what we're talking about.

Fabiola goes on, "You are such a nice person. Maybe too nice . . ."

I blow out a frustrated sigh. Rebel has made the same comment, over and over. And over.

". . . don't get angry. I want to say to you, you are good enough being you. We like it when you're you. If you've changed your hair for yourself, to explore new ideas, that's beautiful. But remember, we know all about the drama going on with you and Adolpho and Mr. Mackie. Please don't change because it's what they want you to do."

"It's not just them," I say, lowering my voice and looking around conspiratorially. "My parents want me to change, too. Dad is so focused on my future that all he sees is the opportunity, the exposure I could get by being here until ninth grade."

"All our parents want us here for the opportunity," Taj says. His tone is firm but gentle. "My father spent a summer trying to be a Cuban rock star back in the Stone Age, and he thinks if he just pushes hard enough, I'll live out all his dreams—but better."

Fabiola and Benz both nod.

"My parents are horrified that I want to be an artist," Fabiola says. Her tiny smile causes her right cheek to dimple. "My mother is a banker. My father works for big business. One day I may actually care enough to know exactly what he does." The tiny smile spreads.

Her smile makes us all smile. She goes on, "But as much as I love art, I have a plan, too. I want an MBA and to work in international finance. Once I've made my first million, then I'll take more time for my art."

I sit back in my seat. I'd never have guessed it.

"All I'm saying," Fabiola went on before diving back into her spaghetti, "is no matter who's breathing down your neck, your future is yours. It would be nice if everything just magically happened just the way you'd like, but sometimes you have to work for it. Do you want to be a professional musician your whole life?"

I have no answer.

Truth is, I've never really thought about it. I'm good at music; Dad encourages me to practice and get better, and teachers are impressed by my talent. Up until now, it has always come easily.

But the rest of my life?

I'm not even sure what I want for the rest of the week!

⚜

The real test comes the next day—Wednesday, the day of the conference. All day long I feel queasy. My compromised hair is tied back prettily with a pink ribbon. My throwback style today goes way back—nubby pink short-sleeved sweater, black-and-white-plaid high-water pants, and authentic, highly polished saddle shoes.

Mom told me she'd meet me in the office at four, just before the meeting. She and I haven't had a real conversation in days.

Then again, we don't really have many real conversations. Our "thing" is smiling and making everything seem okay—always. I thought that was normal, even good. Now, though, it feels messed up.

When I was nine, I remember being fearless. I'd battle

bullies who tried to pull my hair while I did yoga during recess. I convinced our fourth-grade teacher that allowing me to sit crisscross on top of my desk really was good for my back. I bravely accepted that Daddy was never coming back to live with us—and that was okay. Less yelling.

At nine, I was strong, determined, brave.

But somewhere along the way, I began drifting. I didn't want Mom to feel sad; didn't want Daddy to feel sad. My teachers, my friends, Granny—I made myself feel responsible for everyone. And I became convinced the best thing I could do was stay chill, avoid conflict, and keep smiling!

I feel none of that chill/goodwill when, at the end of day, the bell rings and I drag my sorry behind to the front office. Mom stands in front of the counter sticking one of those "My Name Is _____" tags to the front of her business suit. She already has a deer-in-the-headlights look in her eyes.

Normally, seeing her like that would automatically flick my protective switch, but instead I stifle a yawn. Could it be that I've used up my reserve tank of fake cheer?

We make tense smiles at each other, then Mr. Mackie ushers us down the hall to one of the glass-enclosed conference rooms.

Before we even enter, I see what is happening and stop dead in my tracks.

16

Adolpho Cortez is present. So are his parents. The three of them appear so highly polished and doll-like they could be posing for a Christmas catalog.

Somehow Mr. Mackie had failed to mention that the Family Cortez would be present for my conference. Why are they?

Just looking at the four of them—the doll family and Mr. Mackie—I can feel that something is up.

When I shoot Mom a worried glance, she's too busy fidgeting—tugging at the bottom of her suit coat, folding and unfolding the slick backing she'd taken off her sticky name tag, and pressing her lips tightly together in a nervous smile.

An ache starts inside me. My pulse beats in time with a metronome on Mr. Mackie's desk.

It feels like something unexpected had already been decided. But what?

Whether I'm ready for it or not, their conspiracy is lurking there inside the room. Waiting to pounce.

Will I be able to handle what they throw at me next?

I hold my breath as I wait to find out.

❀

The meeting starts off well enough, tight-lipped politeness and words of insincere greeting—"Nice to meet you!" and "Nice to meet you, too." Mr. Mackie explains that Mrs. Cortez is here as a representative of the school board. Great.

My eyes tick from face to face. Adolpho's cheeks are red, but he doesn't look smug or angry, like normal. It's different. He seems as uncomfortable as Mom.

Dr. Cortez is the picture of the modern professional woman. Her rich brown hair is upswept and shellacked to her skull. Her eyelashes are respectably fake. Her makeup flawless. And her eyes are as cold and hard as the diamond sparkling on her finger.

Meanwhile, Mr. Cortez fails at discreetly looking at the screen of his phone. For some reason, he wore his white hospital coat. His name is embroidered on the pocket. His dark expression remains unreadable. A stethoscope hangs uselessly around his neck.

It's easy to understand why Mr. Mackie, in his neat though ill-fitting blue suit, has chosen this room instead of his office. Its bright, floor-to-ceiling windows letting sun paint the space. Brightly colored expensive chairs in orange and yellow and teal surround the glass-topped conference table. Aquatic watercolor paintings splash across stark white walls. It is a chic space.

I see Mrs. Cortez cut a mean side-eye at her husband. He slides his iPhone into a pocket in his immaculate doctor's coat. Beside him, his wife sits up rigidly. They never look directly at each other. Never touch.

That makes me wonder about the "perfect family" image they are clearly pushing on others. Are they as solid as they want to appear?

Once the polite words fade, the doll woman turns to me and says:

"I hear you are a very good violinist. May I ask, how did you learn to play so well?" Her question throws me. I look at Mr. Mackie. Then at Adolpho. Both refuse to meet my gaze. In the back of my mind, I heard the ominous tones of F and F-sharp alternate. *Jaws.* Two notes that became a movie classic. I try to brace myself.

"What does that have to do with anything?" I ask softly. I'm not trying to be confrontational. I'm confused.

"Lotus, don't be rude!" Mom hisses in my ear.

"It's all right, Mrs. Bloom," Mrs. Cortez says with a mock grin. "I know that kids will be kids. It's all in how you raise them."

Mom stiffens beside me.

Then Mrs. Cortez turns her full face to me and says, "I ask because for some reason you've come here and have leaped past other students. Deserving students. My Adolpho, for example, has been taking private lessons since he was six . . ."

"I started lessons at four," I say, not letting her finish. "I began playing at three."

An eyebrow arches with all the venom of an approaching cobra. She looks like she is fighting for control. Ready to strike out with her lethal brow.

Mom jumps in, her voice sounding almost apologetic. "Her father is a professional musician. Lotus was learning piano notes before she could walk. He always made sure music was a huge part of her life."

"Well," begins Mrs. Cortez, "I see."

Mr. Mackie clears his throat.

"Ladies, let's all stay on topic. We are here to discuss disruption in the classroom and the state of Miss Bloom's appearance, which I'm proud to see she has fixed," Mr. Mackie says. Fixed. I've *fixed* myself, like some broken toy.

The unaccustomed itch of anger scrubs at my neck like a turtleneck two sizes too small. He is oblivious. His fingers drumming beside the *tick-tick-tick* of the metronome with its silver balls. He looks as out of place in this fancy space as a dog's water bowl.

"Yes, the hair," Mrs. Cortez says. She sits back in her seat, draws in a breath, and lets it out. I do the same.

I am trying to conjure all the *woo-saaah* on the planet. I feel a shift in the tide and know I need to be ready to ride the current.

"It is a . . . uh, decent effort you have made," she begins, "but how can we be sure you won't turn around and go right back to what you had before. We've put a lot of time, thought, and expense into creating this school's orchestra. Appearance matters. If you revert back to some other primitive style, distractions are inevitable."

"Primitive!" I shout, leaping to my feet. Mom immediately pulls me back into my seat.

As unlikely as it seems, Mom speaks for the first time.

"Don't worry, ma'am, both my husband—ex-husband—and I have spoken with Lotus. She understands the rules and has assured me that she is committed to this *compromise*," Mom says.

Ma'am? Really?

"Well, Lotus has taken a good first step in cleaning up her messy hair," Mrs. Cortez says, her glamorous lips parting for a look-at-me smile, "but is it enough for the image we want for our orchestra? Particularly, our concertmaster."

Both her husband and her son glance at her. Mr. Mackie clears his throat again. So, everyone here knows what she just said was wrong, right? Or is it just me?

"Now, Mrs. Cortez, we only agreed that she needed to fix her hair to follow our dress code," he says.

I've had enough. I blurt, "A dress code that does not take into account that Black girls have Black girl hair. I wear my hair in an afro as a symbol of pride. I like it. Love it. It makes me feel good!"

My chest heaves with a percussive rhythm. What is

happening? What is happening? Why isn't Mom jumping to my defense? Why did catering to the Cortezes matter more than my feelings to her?

"You made a false claim against my son because of a disturbance *you* created!" she says in a fake sugary tone, and I realize Splenda's got nothing on her.

"He's the one who, with his friends, started throwing paper *at me*," I pant, practically bouncing in my seat. She looks at her nails. From her side, I see those carefully painted lips tug into an insincere smile. I keep going: "And he's the one who was sending those awful videos to me and the entire school."

The doll woman flinches. Mr. Mackie sits forward.

"What videos?" asks Mr. Mackie.

Now Adolpho begins to squirm. "Not videos. Memes. It was just meant as a joke, no big . . ."

He doesn't finish because his mother makes a slashing motion at him. Adolpho drops his head. His feet tap faster than the table's metronome. The room draws a deep breath.

Now the doll woman turns her diamond stare toward me.

"That was just simple horseplay provoked by your lack of etiquette, Miss Bloom. No, I think we need better assurance that you won't go back to wearing your hair in that manner. Perhaps some sort of contract. Something that says in writing that you are forbidden from wearing your hair like that again. You could be such an attractive girl, with proper grooming. The twists, well, they are an improvement, but . . ."

Mr. Mackie begins clearing his throat again. "Mrs., uh, Dr. Cortez, you cannot ask a student to sign a contract. It would not be permissible to the administration . . ."

"Then you need to make it permissible. I will not sit here with this . . . this . . . person hurling damaging accusations against my son. And I will not sit quietly by and watch as she erodes everything we spent years fundraising to build into . . ."

"I am not cutting my hair!" I yell, before she evens stops talking.

But Mrs. Cortez isn't done. Drilling me with her icy glare, she says, "As concertmaster, you have a responsibility to present yourself in a certain manner, yes?" Her fake question goes unanswered. "And to keep control of your orchestra. I saw you at the open house. You play well, but your hair was a major distraction that night. It was hard to focus on your beautiful work with that hair in the way. Not just to me, but for several other people who noticed it, as well."

My lips go numb, and I feel ice press into my veins. I've been trying to take deep breaths to remain calm, but I'm starting to sound like a Lamaze class for expectant mothers.

I look at Mr. Mackie, doing his best to ignore this unhinged woman altogether. But I need him to do more.

And the Cobra isn't finished, not yet. Now the tune switches from merely menacing to downright killer. The shower scene. *Psycho.*

"And then there is the maestro's decision to choose you over my Adolpho to recommend for the International Youth

Orchestra. How would that look, Miss Bloom, sending someone so unkempt to Paris?"

I can't help myself. I jump to my feet again, this time snatching away my wrist when Mom grabs it.

"What is wrong with you? I am not 'unkempt.' And I'm not cutting my hair!" I spin to Mr. Mackie and repeat, "I'm not cutting my hair. I'm not even sure I want to keep wearing these dopey twists!"

Mr. Mackie stands, saying, "Let's settle down."

And Mrs. Cortez glides to her feet, pointing an I-told-you-so nail in my direction.

"See! What did I tell you? The problem is greater than her hair. These Black girls from where she's from—MacArthur Park, right?—are volatile. What if she snaps during one of the performances and goes off on another unsuspecting student?"

"Mrs. Cortez, there's no . . . ," Mr. Mackie begins, but she isn't listening.

"No, it should be simple enough for even someone like her to understand. Either she can step down as concertmaster or"—the next words flow out in slow motion—"she must agree to cut her hair!"

The gasps moved around the room.

I want to S C R E A M.

Mr. Mackie looks like he's swallowed a stapler.

"Lotus, I would like to talk to you in my office tomorrow, alone," he is saying.

Then to my total surprise, Mom stands.

"Lotus and I have nothing further to say. My daughter will not be cutting her hair or making any other changes to herself. We are leaving, Mr. Mackie. You don't need to talk to her. You need . . . you need to get your house in order," she says. "Come on, baby. Mama is ready to go."

Mr. Cortez and Adolpho have slid down in their chairs as though they are trying to hide among the woolen fibers of the seat cushion. Mr. Cortez leans away from his wife like she is radioactive.

He might be right.

Refusing to back down, Mrs. Cortez, that doll-faced cobra-woman, pins me with her dark, glittering cobra eyes. She says, "Of course, if you are unable to adapt to the structure and expectations of this type of school, you can always go back where you came from. Our steering committee at the hospital is considering making a generous donation to MacArthur for its music department. Maybe you'd be happier there?"

Needles poke at my face, my lips from the inside. Blood is draining from my head, leaving me light-headed.

"Lotus!" Mom says. Her voice sizzles like a live wire across a stormy road.

"Mrs. Bloom, please . . . ," Mr. Mackie tries again.

But we are out the door.

Out of the school.

And into the salty sea air.

Mom has linked arms with me, her body rigid. She is vibrating and carries me along on a rolling wave of anger I've never seen in her.

"Mom?" I'd wanted her on my side, but her shift in attitude is scaring me.

She swallows hard, then steels herself.

"That woman is the devil!" she says.

"Mom, what . . . what am I going to do?"

"You're not signing some ridiculous contract. You're not going back to MacArthur, unless that's what you want. And you are definitely *NOT* cutting your hair, I know that. That's what you're *not* going to do!"

17

Streaks of orange and magenta thread the evening sky. Purple bleeds through the horizon, turning it into a mosaic. After Mom and I get home, I leave to take a walk and wind up at the beach.

She wanted to talk. I didn't.

By the time I reach Ocean Drive, a lot of the anger has died down. So has my energy. A few bench seats facing the ocean are empty. It isn't quite dark enough to turn the day into a shadowy twilight. But I can tell it won't be long.

When I spot a shadowy figure on one bench, I pause.

Something about the tilt of the head, the curves of the face, immediately brings "When the Saints Go Marching In" to mind. Only one person reminds me of that spirited classic of the French Quarter in New Orleans.

"Dion?" I say softly, questioning myself as much as anything.

When the figure turns, magenta-gold light slashes his features. The half smile is unmistakable. But the tired, weary look in his eyes is new.

"Muse!" he says, lacking all his normal over-the-topness.

I move closer to him. I ask, "Are you all right?"

His shrug looks as worn down as I feel.

"Ahh, you know. Some days are better than others," he says.

For some reason, that simple phrase brings a hot bead of tears to my eyes. He sits up. Concern overtakes his expression.

"Hmm . . . baby girl, I guess the question is, are *you* okay?"

I answer with a dry laugh that does not sound at all like me. "Like you said, some days really are better than others. Today is not one of the good ones," I say.

He nods and pats the seat beside him on the bench.

"Come sit and we can depress each other with our tales of woe." I do as he asks, and for several minutes we sit there, our shoulders not quite touching, our focus on the waves slipping onto shore, then washing out to sea again.

"Your conference was today." It's a statement, not a question. I nod but say nothing.

Dion springs unexpectedly to his feet. He turns his face away from the ocean. In the shadowy light of evening, it is impossible to tell if the smudges beneath his eyes are due to the disappearing daylight or . . . tears.

The smile that flickers over his lips looks painful for him.

He says, "Tell you what. I think we could both use huge ice cream cones. For medicinal purposes, of course. I would say you are a rum raisin kind of girl. Or maybe rainbow sherbet?"

I give a quick, short snort of laughter.

"Rum raisin. I have money," I say, leaning forward to take money from my pocket. But he's already walking away, shaking his head.

End-of-season tourists snap photos. Lovebirds on their honeymoons; snowbirds down from Canada. It isn't quite winter up north, but it's only a matter of time before the beach is filled with snowbirds—what we call people who come down during the winters to bake until turning beet red on the sand.

For now, however, we have the lush autumn air blowing off the ocean and through our hair.

Our hair.

It reminds me that according to Dr. Cortez, my natural hair is "primitive." I shake it off. A mixture of anger and resentment still burn hot in my belly when I think of her.

So instead, I focus on the beauty that lies around us. Neon lights the coming night, highlighting the Art Deco buildings and funky array of tourists and locals moving along the street.

Dion is back quickly. He hands me a cone and sits beside me with his own—dark chocolate with almonds.

We eat in silence. I'm trying hard to settle myself enough to think clearly.

Then Dion says, "Today is my oldest brother DeMarcus's birthday. He would have been twenty-four." When he turns to face me, I understand that the smudges did come from crying. Tears shimmer in his eyes.

I don't know what to say.

"I'm so . . . so sorry." I mean it, even if it is a useless thing to say.

Dion nods slowly.

"He really got me. Only person in the world who I knew, no matter what, always had my back. The world feels lonely without him."

I blink away the tears that are forming in my own eyes. I don't know what it feels like to lose a sibling. I haven't lost anyone, really.

But I know what it's like to feel alone. In that conference room, I felt more alone than any time in my life. Mom's angry display had surprised me. I hadn't expected it and didn't really understand what it meant.

I take Dion's hand into mine and give his fingers a squeeze.

"Tell me what I can do for you," I say.

We kiss cones together. I get a smudge of his chocolate, and he gets a dab of rum raisin.

"Just sit here and be my friend," he says.

And so, I do.

Dion tells me all about his brother.

As he talks, I realize it is the first time I've heard Dion's voice without all the *extra* going on. He says his brother had been a band geek and a baseball player who left high school to join the air force.

I feel myself suck in a breath, thinking I know where the story is going. That he was somehow killed in combat. I've known a lot of kids who had parents or uncles, even aunts, who'd died while serving in the military.

"DeMarcus was home on leave, visiting Miami two years ago when he was killed outside a gas station. Just standing there, pumping gas one minute, then two dudes bum-rushed him, trying to rob him, got mad 'cause he didn't have any cash. Shot him."

Dion's tone is flat and emotionless. Like he's spoken the words a thousand times—in his head and out loud.

I look at him, but he holds his face toward the ocean. He's struggling to hang on. I squeeze his fingers tighter.

Then he gets a little smile and I see just a flicker of the old Dion. He says, "So, princess, what's bringing you down today? That ridiculous conference with the even more ridiculous Mr. Mackie?"

When I frown and lean back, getting a good look at him, he blows out a breath and laughs.

"Ha! Girl, everybody heard you had met to talk about that sad individual, Adolpho, and his robot parents. Did they make him give some fake apology? Something like that?"

It is my turn to blow out a tired laugh, which holds no humor at all. I take a mouthful of ice cream, swallow. I wipe my mouth with a napkin.

"Well, almost, except in the real-life version, his mother wanted me to sign a contract saying I wouldn't wear my afro—or quit concertmaster if I didn't comply. If I didn't agree, she said I could go back to MacArthur where I belong," I say.

I can't match his earlier flat tone. The whole scene is still too raw. The words hurt coming out.

It's Dion's turn to lean back and stare at me, open mouthed.

"Say *what*?"

"Yep," I say. "Changing my hair like Mr. Mackie said wasn't good enough. It was humiliating, the way she talked to me. And even more insulting and embarrassing."

"What did your mama have to say?" he asks.

That brings a whisper of a smile to my lips.

"I have to say, she surprised me. Me and her, we're not confrontation people . . ."

"Well, no duh!" he says.

I shove him, and we both laugh.

"But that woman was so rude and mean that even Mom stood up and walked out. And even though she's been on me for *years* to get rid of my 'fro, she told them I was not cutting my hair or making any other changes. After that, we walked out!"

"Go ahead, then, Mama!" he says.

It doesn't take long before I realize something: I don't feel quite so alone. Mom did have my back. When it really, really mattered.

"Old lizard-face Mrs. Cortez needs to go have an extended spa day—or at least get the stick out of her butt!"

"Shut up!" I say, a bark of laughter bursting from me. Then I sigh. "To be honest, I just don't know what to do. All this conflict and hard feelings, it's not me. I'm a *woo-saaah* kind of girl. Not a fight-the-power kind of girl. I feel so lost, like a flute playing in the violin section."

Dion sits back against the bench. He's quiet for a long moment. We listen to the chorus of waves singing onto shore. He lets out a deep sigh before turning back to me and tapping my hand with his index finger.

"Listen, I've got some real talk for you. You're a young Black woman in a world with a blueprint made by white men. Nothing against white men. Love 'em to death. But chiiiiiile, life won't get easier. Especially for someone as talented as you."

I sigh. "But why can't it be, like, I give all my time and energy to my work and I love what I do? Why can't that be enough?"

He shakes his head.

"I'm still a little mad that you twisted your hair when you didn't want your hair twisted," he says. Then he sharply claps his hands together in my face. "Girl, I mean this with the most respect, but you gotta wake up! You can't just be sitting around waiting for everything to be how you need it to be. Why do you think I'm usually so loud and so over the top?"

"Um, because that's your personality," I say.

"No!" He shakes his head. "I need to come here some-times to clear my head. To feel the quiet, the peace. It's exhausting, always being *on*. Some days I just don't feel up to it. But I do it to make people *have* to pay attention. It's so easy to look right past somebody like me. 'Oh, he's gay, he's extra, he's whatever . . . ,' to just treat me like I don't matter.

"If I sat around trying desperately to stay in my lane, I'd get walked over, talked over, and looked over. But when I come to school cutting up, wearing glitter in my hair and enough eye kohl to shame Nefertiti, oh, honey, somebody gonna pay attention to me."

The darkening sky paints more shadows across his face. Passing headlights light his expression. I just looked at Dion as being . . . Dion. Loud, proud, brassy, and sassy. I never looked any further than that.

But here he is telling me that his behavior is devised to make sure he isn't overlooked. And I'm going around smiling and keeping the peace, and all that really does is make it easy to be overlooked:

Oh, don't worry about Lotus, she'll go along with anything just to make everyone happy!

Still, I think my situation is different.

"Don't you think, though, our situations are not so much alike? I mean, you want people to notice you; I just want everybody to be happy and groove to the music, feel my vibe," I say, doing a little dance in my seat. I suddenly wish I'd brought my violin.

"It's getting dark," he says, "come on. I'll walk back with you to your hood."

Once we are up and crossing Ocean Drive, we head up a side street toward Collins. Dion pulls a face and looks at me.

"Lotus, you don't honestly believe that, do you? That you just want to fit in? Because, girl, nobody struts around here with a three-foot afro and psychedelic pants from the '70s if all they want is to be left alone. You like attention. The question is, are you willing to fight to get the kind of attention and make the kind of impact you want?"

Well, that gives me something to think about.

🪷

And after I get home, there's more to consider.

The house is empty. Mom's note says she's at the market. I feel exhausted and fall asleep almost immediately with a night full of shadowy dreams.

Dad calls at six the next morning, FaceTime. I ignore him. Instead of yoga, I use the dawn hour to undo my twists.

Dion's "real-talk" session had burned inside me during the night.

Did I have everything all figured out? No!

But what was clear was that it was time to stop waiting for a solution and create one myself. At first, I'd thought that being at the Atlantis School was a dream come true and more important than anything. Now I know I was wrong.

Trying to be someone else—that was worse than anything.

Mom is in the kitchen when I come out of my room. I want her to see my hair. I realize I want her approval.

"You took them down?" she says.

I chew the inside of my lip and nod. That woman, Mrs. Cortez, made it sound like I was just running around with my head uncombed and uncleaned. But my hair is long, and getting the rounded afro look is work.

"Mom, I can't . . . I have to do this," I say.

She nods once, then looks down.

"I hope you know what you're doing," she says with a tired sigh.

I frown.

"I thought you were on my side?" I say.

"Lotus, I'm always on your side. I'm your mother. I . . . well, just because I don't think it's right for them to try to make you cut your hair, I don't know if rubbing that woman and the school's nose in it is the way to go. What's going to happen when you go back to school with your twists gone and your hair picked out?"

"I'm going to have my pride back," I say. "I'm going to be able to recognize myself again. Mom, I gotta go!"

I don't want to fight. Don't have time to, really. I have other songs to sing.

Still, I feel jumbled inside about what to do and how to do it. A timpani drum pounds in my chest as I walk to Fourth and Michigan and wait. I need to apologize to someone.

It isn't long before Rebel rounds the corner. She's wearing earbuds and bouncing her head to a rhythm only she can hear. When she sees me her head bounces up.

"Lo!" she calls, and does her goofy run toward me.

I suck in a deep breath. This is either going to be great, or a painful concert of I-told-you-so's.

"What's up, what's up, what's up?" she says. "I haven't talked to you in a bit. Everything good?"

After sucking in another gulp of air, it is time to let it out.

"Not exactly," I say.

Then I tell her.

We walk and talk and stop several times, but I get it out. And then her head nearly explodes off her shoulders.

Literally!

"Are you freaking kidding me with this?" Rebel shouts above the hum and groan of morning traffic.

"I wasn't going to tell you at first because you'd been so ticked off about me planning to twist or change my hair. But I'm sorry, I did it. I did it because I figured it would keep the peace," I say.

Rebel is bobbing her head. "Mmm-hmm! Lo, I've told you—give some people an inch and they try to be a ruler. Keeping the peace is good, but fighting for your rights is better!"

She was born too late. Dr. Martin Luther King Jr. could have used somebody like her on his street team. Then again, she was probably more of a Malcolm X, *by any means necessary* kind of girl.

"I'm really-really-really sorry, Rebel. Sorry that I didn't stand up for you and your fight to get better equipment and maintenance for MacArthur. I'm sorry that I've been so comfortable staying out of things and afraid to . . . to stand up for myself or anyone else."

Rebel drops her book bag and gives me a big hug. She hops around until soon I'm hugging and hopping, too.

"Lotus, I've known you since you were four. I always knew that'd be tough for you. But I'm so glad to hear you say that, stand up for yourself. They can't treat you that way. How dare that boy's mama try to make you cut your hair," she says. "And I'm proud of how you handled yourself."

"Look, I've got to get to school," I say, suddenly feeling shy and maybe unworthy of her praise.

"Yeah, me too," she says, looking down at the time on her phone. "But we'll get together after school. The next rally is Tuesday. We need to strategize. I'm going to text Connor. Maybe he can meet up with us after school."

"It'll have to be late. I have orchestra rehearsal after

school for the holiday show," I say. Part of me is relieved, but I'm already feeling overwhelmed again. I'd been itching to share it with her because I wanted her to tell me what to do. But now that she's ready to jump in and "help," I still feel off balance.

My phone beeps.

Mom.

I wave goodbye to Rebel.

Mom's text reads:

I love you.

I send her a heart emoji and try to prepare myself for the day ahead.

18

School is something out of Weird World News.

My hair is the subject, and everyone has an opinion.

. . . hey, the woolly mammoth is back . . .

. . . take a picture with me, I'll tag you . . .

. . . his mama must be something . . .

. . . that Cortez clique . . . a lot of nerve, yo . . .

In orchestra, the rumors spread fast. Several kids ask, "Is it true? Adolpho's mom tried to have you suspended for wearing your afro? That's why you changed your hairstyle?"

Variations of the question get asked throughout the morning. By lunch, the seventh grade is in a frenzy. Everybody has a theory, a perspective, something.

At first, no lie, it feels exciting. However, when Adolpho and a few of his friends enter the café and immediately get paper airplanes zinged toward their heads, I get a bad feeling.

Adolpho's red face looks around angrily. I'm sitting with Fabiola, Dion, Taj, and Benz. We all look up in time to see the planes flying in from everywhere.

The room goes silent, then there is an eruption of laughter.

"Serve 'em right," says Benz. "Adolpho been a bully since grade school, man. Him and his vampire mama. I was a third grader, and he was in fifth. Him and his buddies were always taking my lunch money. When we reported it, he told the teacher *I* was the one stealing his money. And his mother came to the school and demanded I apologize or face getting kicked out."

"What did you do?" asks Taj, dropping a row of sizzling hot fries into his mouth. Instantly, he burns his tongue and starts going, "... *hot, hot, hot,*" and all of us crack up.

"One at a time, Taj," Fabiola says in her posh French-Creole accent.

"But, yeah, what did you do?" I ask.

"I apologized. Man, that still bothers me to this day. Every time I see his smug face I want to smack him with something." He steals three of Taj's fries.

"Hey!" Taj protests.

Benz wags a fry at me. "Don't let them push you around. If you do, you'll regret it, just like I did. Freaking Cortez bullies!"

I remain silent while the boys play tug-of-war with the french fries. After a few seconds pass, Fabiola leans into me.

"Even though he does not have enough sense not to talk with potato and ketchup in his mouth, Benz may have a point. I think standing up for your rights is the only thing you can do. You've done nothing wrong," she says.

Then it's Taj's turn. He swallows a lump of fries, takes a swig from his orange Hi-C. He says, "But right now you've been chosen to represent us in the International Youth Orchestra. If you get suspended or kicked out of school, you could jeopardize that."

I gulp down my mouthful of salad. It seems to knot up in my throat. I take several deep breaths before I speak, afraid I'll spray the table in secondhand greens.

"Believe me, I've considered that. Every time I convince myself I have to fight, I think about what it'll feel like to have to give up my spot in that orchestra to someone else. Especially if it's Adolpho!"

Everyone is silent after that.

Then a disembodied voice echoes off the walls. *"Will Lotus Bloom please come to Dean Mackie's office? Lotus Bloom . . . "*

Okay, remember on the first day of orchestra? When I was sent from beginning orchestra to main and expected everyone to stop what they were doing like it was high noon in some old Western?

Yeah, well, it didn't happen then—but it's happening now!

I can feel everyone's gaze. Eyes crawling over me. A mixture of amusement and curiosity behind their stares. Even a little awe.

When I stand and grab my things, Benz tugs one of my wrists.

"Remember, Afro, stand strong. You got this!" He grins and gives me a fist bump. The others raise their fists one by one, each giving me a bump.

Avoiding eye contact with Mercedes and her set is impossible. They are all gaping at me. Feeling the power of the flower, I toss the woolly mammoth in all her glory, turn directly to face them, and blow a kiss. Then I turn and walk straight ahead to the door, trying to block out the roar of comments, laughter, jeers, and cheers that follow beneath the peaked dome of the café atrium.

The secretary tells me to go right in as soon as I arrive. When I walk in, Mr. Mackie is nervously running his hands through his hair, then drumming a tuneless rhythm on his desk.

And the Cobra is seated in a chair across from him. Along with two other women, equally slicked, with matching glares and lethal eyebrows.

"Miss Bloom, please come in, take a seat," he says, half standing when I enter.

I pull the seat out and slowly sink into it. My back is stiff, and I force myself to maintain eye contact. My insides are a boiling witches' cauldron of emotion. I'm expecting him to be volcanic. To be angry. To launch a tirade.

Instead, he looks tired, and frustrated.

"Miss Bloom . . ." His voice comes out on a puff of air. An exhale that blows from the center of this man's soul. I shudder at that exhale. "I thought we had an understanding. Why have you gone back on your word?"

Mr. Mackie is an assortment of nervous tics and twitches—tapping his foot, drumming his fingers, tugging at the red tie the color of tomato soup. He and I both are making an effort not to make eye contact with the women.

"Yes, Miss Bloom. I thought we had your word," Mrs. Cortez says coolly.

"I can't do it, Mr. Mackie, Mrs. Cortez. I can't. Because what's next? What are you going to demand next?"

He clears his throat. She arches her eyebrows. She and the other women exchange looks. The middle woman, as tall and sleek as Mrs. Cortez, stands. Her white suit and gold jewelry make her look like art.

"Miss Bloom," she begins, and my stiff back becomes stiffer. "My name is Penelope Garcia-Paas. I am an attorney and a member of the steering committee. My son, Ashton Drew, is also a member of the advanced orchestra. A trumpeter. I'm sure you know him."

I slowly shake my head. "I've never heard of him," I say. Because it's true. Ashton Drew?

Her nostrils flare, and her already hard eyes grow even harder. I wonder if Ashton Drew is another paper plane pilot. She blows steam from her delicate, slightly upturned nose and continues:

"I am here to inform you that you are in breach of the school's code of standards and ethics. You do remember

196

signing it when you started the school year, don't you?" She extends her perfectly manicured nails and hands me a folded piece of paper. "You are being served with notice that failure to comply with your original agreement will result in immediate expulsion. You have until Monday!"

The third woman, rounder and softer than Mrs. Cortez or the proud mother of the trumpeter, shifts uncomfortably in her seat. When she stands, I notice her gaze ping from face to face to face.

"Penny, I'm not sure you have the auth . . ."

The poor woman is the victim of a double glare from the other two women.

I feel my knees shaking. Mr. Mackie gulps loudly.

"No, Angel!" snaps Mrs. Garcia-Paas. "I am a concerned parent and a member of the fundraising and steering committee. We have a right to protect the image of our new school and set the tone for what is allowable and what behavior will not be accepted!"

Thin blue veins rise in the woman's throat. It's my turn to gulp.

"Look, Lotus, I'm standing in for Dean Cassius. As you all know, he's due back later this month. My job is to just keep everything rolling smoothly until he gets back." Mr. Mackie sighs heavily. "Lotus, won't you please reconsider? The way your hair was yesterday, the chunky braids, that was pretty, right?" His expression is so hopeful, I almost feel sorry for him.

He looks so miserable I almost consider it. Then Mrs. Cortez, her tone an awful sneer, continues. "Tick-tock, Miss Bloom. You have until Monday. Monday you fix that . . . that mop! Or you give up your space at our school until further notice!"

Our school!

"You . . . they can't do that?" I say. I look wildly between the awful women and Mr. Mackie.

"Ladies!" says Mr. Mackie, looking as wild eyed as me.

"Come on, ladies," Mrs. Cortez says with a sniff. They move in unison toward the door. That Penelope lady in lead and Mrs. Cortez in the rear. She turns back and looks at me, unable to keep from delivering a cheesy parting shot:

"We take our rules very seriously," she says, sounding like a Bond villain.

"Mrs. Cortez! That's quite enough!" says Mr. Mackie. Too little, too late. The three women exit, and I wobble until I drop back into the chair, holding the trifolded piece of paper.

"I'm sorry, Miss Bloom. I'm only filling in. I'm not sure the board or steering committee has the authority to act in such a manner, but I do know that if they are determined to have you expelled, they won't stop until they have exhausted every avenue. I'm truly sorry it has come to this."

Later, at the center, the little boy named Drake holds onto the neck of the violin too tightly. I rub my finger over his. "Not so hard, Drake," I say. "Relax some of the tension in your hand and fingers."

I'm almost at the end of my time with the kids today. They've been quite lively, and normally they make me laugh. But today, I'm too wound up.

"You okay?" Drake asks when he sees me rubbing a kink in my neck. My head has begun to throb above my eye. Too much going on inside my head.

"I'm fine," I say. He's not stupid. He can clearly see that's a lie.

"We're rooting for you, you know," he says.

"Rooting for me how?" I ask him. "Hey, can I get everyone to bring your instruments up front and lay them down."

Ava says, "My sister told me about that boy trying to bully you about your hair. I like your hair. You shouldn't have to wear it different just 'cause he don't like it and his mama don't like it!" Her reedy little voice is a high soprano, but her conviction is strong.

I frown, looking from her face to Drake's and the others'. Drake nods.

"My brother told me, too. He say he don't know you personally, he goes to Freedom Middle, not Atlantis. But he said his friend told him about it. He say you got guts, going up against those rich people. I say you have to fight back against bullies!"

Drake's dark brown eyes flash with emotion as he speaks. All the kids are nodding, and it chokes me up to think they're actually paying attention to this whole ridiculous drama.

Now even the little kids have an idea of what I should be doing. Everyone seems to know—except me!

"Thanks, guys. I appreciate your support. I just want all of this to blow over so life can go back to the way it was."

"That's exactly what you don't want!" booms a familiar voice from the door. We all turn. Here comes Rebel. And she's with her boo.

She is decked out in all black again, a woven map of Africa around her wrist, Bantu knots on her head and black shades on her face. Her light brown skin appears to glow beneath the room's lights and the daylight from the windows.

Beside her, Connor Woods is wearing a black T-shirt that says Fight the Power! His faded, washed jeans are ripped—in an expensive mall-store kind of way, not an I-can't-afford-to-have-clothes-with-no-holes vibe—and his black hair is swept to one side like a K-pop dude's.

"Who is that?" Drake asks.

"My friends, guys. Okay, my group can head out to the common area and wait for your parents to pick you up," I say. As they head for the door, I call out, "And thank you, guys, truly, for the support. I really appreciate it."

Drake pauses in the doorway as Rebel and her boo approach. "Hey, Miss Lotus," he says, "I'm glad you come here to tutor us. This is my favorite time of day!"

"Mine too!"

"Me too!"

"*Meeeee*!"

Several of them poke their heads back inside in agreement. My chest tightens, and instantly I know the feeling. It's love. I've really fallen for the little dudes. And dudettes.

They're barely out the door when Rebel starts in:

"I got your text. Can't believe they're considering expelling you." She turns to Connor. "That's perfect. Right, babe?"

Babe?

"Right," he says. "By the way, forgive *her* manners. I'm Connor."

"I sort of figured that," *babe*! "I'm Lotus. And why is that 'perfect'? What are you two talking about?"

They look back and forth, and for a second, I want to smack them both. Matching expressions that say, *Isn't it obvious*? Hmph! I'm not in the mood.

"There is another school board meeting tomorrow. They've had to shift from Tuesday for a while because of a plumbing issue in their old spot. Anyway, this is perfect. My group is planning a big turnout for the meeting," she says, practically breathless with glee.

I can feel the panic rising in my body. A bout of queasiness grips me. For a few seconds, I think my lunch salad is going to make a special guest appearance. I push it back down. For now.

"Rebel, how does my getting expelled from Atlantis over my afro have anything to do with your fight to get better funding for MacArthur? I don't quite see the connection," I say. I motion for them to join me on the floor. My neck hurts from looking up.

I abandon the strewn music, and we all sit crisscross facing one another.

Connor—who, no offense, I wasn't talking to—speaks first:

"Well, the two cases can be combined because as young Black women, you're both being denied freedom of expression," he says. It takes everything I have not to roll my eyes.

Rebel is nodding enthusiastically, like a bobblehead doll.

"He's right, Lo. So not only has the county robbed us and our neighbors of a quality education—both traditional and musical—but now, they're basically telling you that the only way you can be accepted is by total assimilation!"

I think of the pages from our history book. Mr. Burke talking to us about Sojourner Truth and her rousing speeches on tree stumps. Picturing Rebel as the next groundbreaking pioneer woman fighting for women's rights is one hundred percent imaginable.

Again, the two exchange glances. I know something else is up. What?

"I get the feeling you're plotting something, Rebel," I say.

Her smile starts slow and spreads wide. I glance at Connor, and he's nodding slowly at her. A go-ahead-and-tell-her look on his face. I have the urge to brace myself.

"Okay, Lo, I know how much you hate confrontation, but now is the time to stand up!" says Rebel. Once again she's standing. I'm still on the floor.

"I know that, Rebel."

"Good. Because I have a plan," she says. Oh boy! I gulp hard and make room for what is surely going to be a hard pill to swallow. (Granny used to say that all the time, and I thought she was talking about her medicine.)

"I think you should go to the school board meeting and let them have it. Their lack of funding made you leave the school where you belonged, and look what happened to you! I mean, you're coming back to MacArthur anyway, right? I know you don't want to deal with that oppression anymore!"

"You want me to quit Atlantis?" Now I stand so that we're eye to eye. Well, almost. I'm about two inches taller than her. Connor stands and actually places a hand on my shoulder.

For the first time in my life, I wish I knew karate!

"Listen, Lotus," says good old Connor Woods, "Rebel has a point. We think one way to force them to invest in our— your—schools is to bring back the talented kids the system has stolen."

"Yeah, Lo. They try to convince themselves that our

schools aren't worth saving and nobody there is worthy. You can change that. You can stand up, let them know how they've wronged you, then shove their fancy school down their throats!"

She draws in a deep breath and blows it out.

"And, Lo," she goes on, "you know Atlantis is depriving you of cultural expression, and they're threatening to cut off your educational opportunities. They are threatening your future, girl," Rebel says. Then for emphasis, she smacks her hands with each word. "That. Cannot. Stand!" and "We. Must. Fight!"

They are both bobbing their heads. Clearly, Connor is as caught up in her performance as I am. Still, the sound of squeaking hinges and sight of Uncle Steve in the doorway flood my body with relief.

"Hey, Unk," I call out. Connor turns, and I wave my hand in his direction, saying, "Connor Woods, this is my uncle, Steven Knight. He runs this center."

Connor reaches out, and Unk shakes his hand. "Unk, he's Rebel's *friend*." I put just the right emphasis on "friend." Uncle Steve's eyebrows shoot up.

"Are you *the* Steve Knight? Number forty-four? Linebacker and legend at the U?" Oh, Lord! Connor's eyes take on a familiar glazed expression. It overtakes many people when they meet my uncle, a former football star at University of Miami.

Unk shakes his hand and nods.

"Yes," he says, "one and the same. Now, what's this I hear about a threat to your education? What's up?" He has turned his attention to me, and I get that feeling of being under a microscope.

"You mean she hasn't told you?" asks Rebel. I groan inside.

"I . . ." That's as far as I get.

"The same rich parents who are leeching money from our school have pressured the school to expel her!" Rebel reveals. I swear, she is glowing. Revolution does wonders for the complexion.

Unk frowns. "Expel her? On what grounds?"

By now, the ever-glowing Rebel is nearly levitating.

"On the grounds of being young, Black, and gifted!" she says. When Unk's frown deepens, she says in that same *Don't you understand anything* tone. "Her hair! They demanded she get rid of her bodacious woolly mammoth. She caved, but only for a day. Then she came to her senses and got her groove back, and they are giving her until Monday or they're going to kick her out of their precious . . ."

Unk raises his palm.

"I get the picture, Rebel. Thank you. Lotus, can I talk to you in my office?" I shoot a look at Rebel. She totally overlooks my death glare.

"Okay, Play Uncle, we're going now. Lo, I'll check in with you later so we can continue strategizing for tomorrow. The school board meeting is going to be fi-yeeeeeer!"

Uncle reaches out his hand. He guides me down the hall with him. A few other counselors stop us with questions about kids or pickups. Before long I'm sitting on the small black sofa in his office. His huge body drops into a chair, and he leans with his meaty forearms resting on his legs.

"What's this all about?"

With my hundredth sigh of the day, I begin my tale.

I finish my story—explaining how all I want is to play my music and have everyone get along. How I don't want to pick a fight. I explain how the whole paper airplane thing started, how I tried to avoid it.

I spill it. All of it. Finishing up with today's trip to Mr. Mackie's office and the trio of terror.

"And that's it," I say, feeling like I'm sick of this story and hope I never have to repeat it again. "Now, Rebel and her boo-thang are planning a rally straight out of 1968. I'm expecting Angela Davis and all the Black Panthers to show up." Our media specialist at Bayside taught us all about the Black Panther Movement. She did not mess around.

That earns me a half grin. "I'm proud that you know who Angela Davis and the Black Panthers are. And what's the school's problem with your hair?" he asks.

Now I chew inside my cheek. I feel helpless when one cold tear wedges across the windowsill of my eyelid.

"They seem to think when it's an afro it's 'unkempt.' Do you know how much work I put into looking natural? That takes a lot of work!"

"I do. And what about Rebel? What's going on with her?"

"She seems to think that Atlantis and its afro censorship works right into her plans to prove freedom in the republic is at risk and all mankind is in danger. Or something like that."

He gives me a look.

"Baby girl, why didn't you tell me any of this? You've been coming in here two or three times a week for nearly two months. You didn't think to share this with me?"

His voice sounds hurt. A guilt pain grabs my insides and twists.

"I . . . I'm sorry. I was doing my best to manage it. I never imagined it would turn into all this," I say.

"All what?" he asks. His eyebrows inch upward.

"You know," I practically sputter. "This! Trouble! Rebel is ready to light torches and storm the schoolyard. She wants to storm the school board meeting, make a big splash. She wants me to quit Atlantis.

"Then there are the kids at school. They're all worked up. Now, all these kids are turning against Adolpho and his friends. I don't want that. He's been a jerk, but I never wanted people to mistreat him."

Uncle comes over to the sofa where I'm sitting, reaches over, and wraps an arm around me. "You're a sweet kid. But you still haven't told me—what does *Lotus* want? What do *you* want to see happen?"

I fill my cheeks with air and slowly blow it out until I'm making a raspberry with my lips. We both sort of laugh.

"I want to wear my hair the way I want. I want to be concertmaster. I want . . . I want to perform in the International Youth Orchestra in Paris. And . . ."

He's making a rolling motion with his hands, telling me to keep going.

"And I want to move to Paris with Dad and go to music school there. That's what I want!" There! I'd said it. But . . . oddly, once I say it out loud, I wonder if it's really true. Is that what I really want?

Uncle Steve stands now, crossing his large arms over his body until his huge hands are pinned beneath each arm.

"Does my sister know all this?" he asks.

I shake my head furiously.

"No! And you can't tell her. I'm not ready for that conversation."

"And what about this stuff with Rebel? Her and her— what did you call him? Her 'boo-*thang*'? She wants your help getting some sort of equality or support for the schools where you live. Is that something you want to be part of?"

I can feel the jittering inside me. See, *this* is the problem. I do want to help Rebel. But I don't know how to do it without causing even more trouble for myself at Atlantis.

"She wants me to go to this district board meeting, make a big scene about how the funding issues cause problems for both of us, and quit Atlantis for its unfair practices and 'oppression,' " I say.

"Quit? As in leave the new school? Is that what you want?"

"I go back and forth. I'm so upset and . . . and angry! I try never to let myself get angry, but now that I am, it's got me feeling all turned upside down inside."

Uncle Steve nods. "I'll ask again," he says, "Is quitting Atlantis what you want?"

"I . . . I don't know anymore. I don't like how I'm being treated there, that I can't be myself. But Rebel is so much better at this, at confrontation. Standing up to people," I say. I hear a whine creep into my voice that is so unappealing.

"Maybe it's time for you to get some practice. Look, me and my big sister don't see eye to eye on a lot of things. The way she lets Mama (he means Granny) walk all over her— the way she lets your father walk all over her—it makes me so mad. She's a good person, and she does not deserve Mama's constant negativity. But the worse part of her passivity is seeing how it has affected you," he says.

I droop in my seat. That is not what I need to hear. I already have enough on my mind. Uncle Steve seems to disagree.

"I'm not going to tell you what to do," he says. "I'm proud that you ditched the twists if that's your choice. And I'm glad other people are behind you. But sometimes in life we have to stand up for ourselves, to stand with others. This might be your time."

❧

Later, at home, I lock myself in my room with my violin and Mozart. Just me and Wolfie. I play his Concerto no. 5. I shut my eyes and fold myself between the notes. My bow slices swiftly, capturing the emotion, the joy, the energy.

The world is blue behind my eyes. Swirls like ocean paint the energetic world that takes me away inside the music.

When the piece finally ends and I open my eyes, a single tear rests on my cheek. My heart is hammering.

It's time to make a choice.

It's time to take a stand.

19

I take a long, hot bath with my hair pushed upward and held with a scarf to keep it out of the sudsy water. Taking care of my natural hair is something I've always felt pride in. I picture myself playing music on a bridge in Paris.

I haven't talked to Dad in a week.

We haven't talked about the latest developments or even the developments before the latest developments.

So many conflicting emotions tangle and fight inside my head, I can't figure out what to do.

I think about why I first got interested in Paris. Besides Dad being there.

Back in the early part of the twentieth century, lots of Black artists—musicians, painters, poets, authors—flocked to Paris for its openness to our culture. Would I be a modern-day version of Josephine Baker or James Baldwin? An artistic soul seeking a safe space?

The warm bath and scented bubbles leave me feeling dreamy.

Granny's voice kills the dream.

"What're you doing in there so long?" she asks, scowling. I quickly wrap myself in a robe, the ocean-colored head wrap still supporting my 'fro. She's coming out of the kitchen.

"Hey, Granny. I didn't know you were here," I say for lack of anything else.

"Your mama is starting Weight Watchers again," she says with an eye roll. The walls on my diplomacy fort are cracking.

"Granny, why do you do that?" I say. "Why do you constantly try to make Mom feel bad about herself?"

The question, challenging her at all, is so unlike me, we both wind up blinking at each other like an unfamiliar sun has shone in through the evening sky.

"I'm just trying to help her be better," she finally says. Her voice is surprisingly soft. "Is that what you think? That I'm picking on her?"

I walk toward her, and we both wind up sitting across from each other at the kitchen table.

"Yeah, Granny. I think that's how Uncle Stevie feels, too. I'm sure you don't mean to," I say, not sure if I believe it, "but I know she isn't very confident. I think we could help her with that."

Oh, how many times I've imagined having *this* conversation. Saying *these* words. Always, I've talked myself out of it because I was afraid doing so would create some sort of cosmic rift. I thought confronting the problem would bring more problems. I never realized that there's a certain peace that comes with confronting what's wrong, and making it right for you.

And for the first time in a while, I'm feeling more at peace. Yet, still guarded. A small tickle of doubt scratching below the surface of my calm.

She lets out this long sigh and slumps back into the chair. Suddenly, she looks about ten years older. She rests her face in her hand.

"You know why I pick at you about your hair?" This should be good. "I grew up here. Mama bought this house with money she saved scrubbing and cleaning them fancy hotels. You know she had to have one of her white friends, a lady from the hotel, front for her to get this house?"

I shake my head.

"Sho' did. By the time they realized it belonged to a Black woman it was too late. A few people tried to give her a hard time, but Mama was stubborn. She waited 'em out. She was determined to keep this house. And she did, too!"

"Good for her!" I say.

Granny looks proud. Then the look turns wistful. "But . . . Mama was a hard woman. Guess I take after her in that respect. When I came to her crying because the white kids at my school were picking at me because of my hair being nappy, kinky, she told me my education was more important. She told me to don't come crying every time some white person said something ignorant. She told me to stand up for myself.

"By high school, I was plumb tired of standing up for myself.

213

I started pressing my hair straight as a bone. I met your grandfather. We both dropped out in tenth grade and got married. Chile, we did some of every kind of job. I was lucky. I didn't get pregnant with your mama for almost fifteen years. By then, I didn't think I could get pregnant. Know what's funny?"

I shake my head. Granny never opens up like this. It's amazing to hear her doing so now. She goes on, "Me and your granddaddy was renting this shabby little house up in Lauderdale. I gave birth to your mama right there in the house. Outside the window was the most beautiful tree. I loved that tree."

"What kind?" I ask, thinking I already know the answer.

She smiles. "A willow tree. I called her Willa Jean 'cause back then I'd never heard of no Black girl name of Willow before."

We both laugh.

Granny sighs. "I know Stevie has always thought I was too hard on your mama. He's ten years younger than her, but he's super protective. I love Willow with all my heart." She reaches out and grabs my hand. "I love both my girls. I consider you my girl, too. I look at you and see myself, only younger."

I smile.

"You called her 'Willow' instead of 'Willa Jean.' You never call her that."

"Maybe; I guess I should. I just want her to have more choices than I did. Time goes by so fast, Lotus. So fast. One minute you're young with all these plans, then the next thing you know"—she snaps her fingers—"you're past middle age and life is passing you by. When I came up, the way I came up, Black women, we were like furniture in the background. Even Black men it feels like took great pleasure in getting their white trophy wives and leaving us behind.

"It's so different now. Look at you! In that fancy school showing them folks what you can do. I hope by the time you're my age, you can look back on a life you feel proud of. Don't let life just happen, Lotus. Jump in and do something about it. Don't just let life happen—make it happen. That's what I want for you. An intentional life!"

Morning comes too swiftly. I awaken early, still thinking about Granny. The talk we had yesterday made me happy— but at the same time, it almost made me angry.

Happy, because it was good to hear her speak so openly. Listening to her talk about the struggles of being a young Black woman reminds me of our continued struggle to be heard, to be valued, to be relevant.

Angry, because I feel like if me and Mom weren't always trying to avoid confrontation, it's a talk we could've been having for years.

Mom offers to cook breakfast for me. I'm up early enough and it's something we haven't done in a while, sit and eat breakfast together.

"Sure," I say. "Be out in a sec. I need to talk with you about something, anyway."

She pauses. "Something wrong?" A cloud of worry covers her expression. I didn't tell her about the expulsion letter. Last night, I hadn't had the energy. But I'm going to tell her now.

And I've decided, I'm going on full assault. Somebody get Angela Davis on the phone. I'm tired of whispering what I want. It's time to roar!

Rebel is planning to launch me at the school board meeting like a missile tonight. It's like she wants to wave me in their faces and then yank me back. She wants them to acknowledge my talent but also acknowledge that I wouldn't have to go to a fancy new school if the board would only put resources and money into MacArthur.

"At MacArthur," she told me earlier, "you could be talented with a 'fro, and it would make no never mind!"

Oh boy! I need to be ready.

I fluff my hair and see that it's grown. It's so lush and plush and fabulous. Who could hate this hair?

While I'm drying it with a T-shirt—regular towels can be too rough for naturals—I decide to go a different style route. Sort of Angela Davis 2.0.

I pull out a scarf designed with repeating shapes of Africa. It's not really a scarf, but a long piece of fabric I got at the craft store. I use it to push up the back of my hair into what's called a pineapple. Heaps of curly, soft afro hair is scooped straight up into a glorious waterfall.

It's the kind of style, unlike a normal 'fro, meant to maximize attention. They can't handle the 'fro, well, get ready for Pineapple 'Fro! I laugh to myself, pluck a pair of super large hoop earrings off the dresser, and get to work.

I am dressing for effect.

It's a very '60s vibe, courtesy of the thrift store—brightly colored rectangles, trimmed in black, on a bright white background. A very trippy mini-dress. If only I had a pair of white go-go boots. Ooo! Then I remember. Mom has a pair of white lace-up ankle boots that would look so cool with this. I tiptoe across the hall to her room, root around in the bottom of her closet, and . . .

Académie des Arts de Paris.

The name is printed atop an envelope.

An envelope stuffed in the back of Mom's closet. Suddenly, the pineapple isn't my main concern.

I'd sent away for an information packet and more information regarding their music program and scholarship. Seeing the envelope in here, tucked away at the back of the closet, causes a jolt to my heart.

Why does she have this?

I look around, feeling like a spy on a secret mission. Then I carefully remove the letter. It's short but to the point:

Dear Miss Bloom,

Everything you need to know about our school and our scholarship program is now online. Thank you

for your interest. To answer your question, yes, we do participate in the International Youth Orchestra program, and yes, having that experience may increase your visibility among our candidates.

Good luck with your music education this year, and best wishes to you. Our program is competitive and the scholarships to our school are difficult to acquire, but can be quite rewarding. We welcome talent and wish you all the best.

Je vous prie de croire, Mademoiselle,
en mes sentiments devoues,
Madame Bouvoir

"Lotus! French toast is getting cold!" Mom calls from down the hall. I grab the boots and shove the letter back into its hiding place.

My heart hammers in my chest. I grit my teeth. Part of me wants to retreat, curl up, and ignore everything.

No. I'm not doing that anymore. Now I'm facing my challenges head on. I'm tired of hiding and making excuses.

What does it mean that Mom has this letter and never said anything?

What does it mean that she's hidden it?

I put on the boots, lace them up, and stand. I'm going to find out.

At least I feel confident about my style this morning. But

as my newly formed resolve is to do as Granny urged last night and live with meaning and intention, I decide soon as I fess up my news, I'm going to ask about the letter.

However, when I enter the kitchen, drawn by the double whammy of warm cinnamon and butter, I stop short.

A strange woman is at the back door, one foot inside. There's someone behind her. A man. Mom is looking back and forth over her shoulder like she's on a game show and looking for a lifeline.

"Mom?" I say. She glances up at my hair.

"Lotus!" Mom says my name on a whoosh of relief. "Lotus, this is . . ."

"I'm Sally. Sally Bird, WSVN Channel 7 News," the woman says, taking this opportunity to push her way into my kitchen. Only then do I realize there is more than one other person with her.

Before me or Mom can react, a cameraman, a man with a mic wearing a fuzzy gray hat on a pole, and a woman carrying a clipboard are all crowding into our kitchen.

The short, redheaded clipboard woman says her name is Carol. "We're sorry to barge in like this, but we were hoping to catch you ladies at home before you left this morning," she says.

Sally, seeming to feel some type of way because Carol spoke over her, pouts her perfectly glossed pink lips and jumps in:

"I cover schools and education, and I've been following

the story of the MacArthur students protesting the state of their school," she says in a tone I just know she's practiced. Very *news-at-eleven*.

The reporter wedges herself even farther into our home and continues:

"Rebel Mitchell, the organizer of the movement to improve conditions at MacArthur schools, tells us that you've been having trouble at Atlantis—being threatened with expulsion if you don't get rid of your—might I say, beautiful—afro, by Monday. Doesn't that treatment prove her point? That the needs of African American students are being ignored while other groups are benefiting. So the question is, why can't MacArthur schools get improvements for their community, too?"

Mom's gasp seems to echo around the room.

Sally and Carol glance at her like they forgot she was here.

I stand there, mouth open for several seconds before finally finding my voice. "Um, why don't you guys head into the living room." I point across the hallway and hang back to grab Mom's hand.

"I was going to tell you at breakfast," I whisper.

"What happened?" she asks, also in a whisper.

"Come on, I'll explain."

Holding hands, we enter our small living room where Sally, Carol, and the crew are already setting up.

Our Miami Beach home was left to Mom from her grandma. It's an old house that Mom has updated here and there. Like many homes from its era, the house is not that big, but the curved archways that sit atop the doorways and the rich, dark hardwood floors make the house feel rich and special.

"Why don't you ladies sit here, on the sofa," Carol says, inviting us to sit in our own living room. Mom's hand trembles in mine, and I squeeze her fingers. After being positioned and repositioned on her oversized, pink floral sofa, Sally is ready.

"Okay, ladies, we're going to just ask you a few questions, no need to be nervous," she says, and I feel my heart rate spike.

Then we begin.

I explain to Sally that I hadn't even had a chance to tell Mom about yesterday's development. The idea of witnesses learning information vital to the story live and on camera seems to give Sally a shiver.

"By all means," she purrs. "Explain it to Mama and our audience."

I see Mom flinch when the woman refers to her as "Mama." I almost laugh. No time for laughing, though.

"Oh, wait!" Carol cries. "Lotus, where's your violin?"

"My bedroom," I say.

"Could you bring it out, please? It would add a great visual to the shot," she says.

I get up, almost stalking down the hall. My phone beeps on my bed. It's Rebel! God, I've never wanted to wring her neck more than I do right now.

Did Sally and her news crew arrive?

So she knew they were coming.

Knew they were coming. Afraid you'd move if you knew in advance. Luv ya!

I'm really going to kill her!

"May I say, you are such a beautiful girl!" coos Carol. "I love the vintage vibe of your style. So retro chic."

I slide onto the couch next to Mom. "Thank you." I reach up and touch my flower. Take a breath. The man with the lights holds some kind of meter near my skin, adjusts me to the light, then we begin.

"We're not live, guys, so relax. We're recording this for the noon news and to lead into our five o'clock slot before the school board meets tonight," Carol says. Mom and me nod.

"Lotus Bloom, tell us about your experience at the new, multimillion-dollar Atlantis School of the Arts," says Sally.

And so . . . I do.

🪷

The interview takes almost an hour. By the time they're done, I'm late for school. Mom drives me, and we talk on the way.

"Soooo," Mom says. We both pause, then we burst out laughing. Mom, who never raises her voice if possible, says, "What in the world was that?"

"One word: Rebel!"

She snorts a laugh. "Like my own mama would say, that girl could pick a fight with a signboard." We both laugh a little before she goes on. "Lotus, baby, why didn't you tell me that awful woman showed up yesterday? How did she even find out your hair wasn't in twists anymore?"

"I suspect her son called her," I say.

"Well, that woman is some sort of terrorist. She had no right to show up and talk to you that way. I'm sorry for that."

"Thanks, Mom, but this time I'm not backing down."

We stop at a light a few blocks away from school. She sighs. "Lotus, I . . . I don't know how this is going to work out. What if you really get kicked out of school? Are you going to be able to live with that?"

"I'm not sure. But I do have a plan. Well, part of a plan. I'm working it out. I've decided I'm not going down without a fight."

I'm holding my breath.

I'm not going down without a fight.

Hard to believe those words came out of my mouth.

"If I have to, I'll go back to MacArthur. At least there I can be me," I say, almost believing I mean it.

Mom walks in with me and signs me in at the attendance office. Orchestra has already begun when I enter. Taking in another gulp of courage, I exhale and head over to Maestro's desk before I take my seat.

"Miss Bloom," Maestro says. He's seated at his desk and

not looking at me. One of the tactics he uses to show his displeasure. I'm not in the mood.

"Maestro, I may get kicked out of school on Monday depending on what happens tonight, so you might have to have Tatiana take over for a while. Maybe for good." The words come out in a rush. Not until it's all out there do I realize I've been holding my breath.

Now I have his full attention. His back stiffens, and he looks up at me like I've suggested we fill the horns with peanut butter.

"What are you talking about? What does this mean?"

Man, I'm so sick of telling this story.

I tell him the story.

He looks at me like I'm radioactive.

"Who are these people who think they can tamper with my orchestra? Who is this woman who thinks she can dictate who is or is not concertmaster in my orchestra?"

Whether he knows it or not, his voice has risen and he's drawing attention. Several kids look over at us. I turn my back to the room. Maestro seems oblivious to the onlookers.

"We shall see who is in charge of this orchestra!" he says. Then he stalks out of the room, leaving me alone at his desk with the eyes of the entire orchestra on me.

When I catch Adolpho's curious gaze on me, I want to scream, *This is all your fault. You and your stupid friends and your stupid paper airplanes and your stupid mother!*

20

The day only gets wilder!

Rumors zip around faster than half notes. Everyone is blaring their version of events. Squawking off-key truths as loud as a brass section. With each retelling of my story, each time I plunge into the *he said, she said* of it all, I get a little angrier.

By lunchtime, my back is straight and my shoulders are stiff with anger. I feel piped up on the collective rage of all the people who think the Cortezes are in the wrong.

Still, the café turns into ground zero.

When I walk in with Fabiola, the room explodes in noise. I'm hoarse already from the telling and retelling of events, and I'm thankful when Fabiola takes over like a press agent and tells people, "No comment."

Noise, loud and sharp like cymbals banging in an elevator, clangs in my ears. My brain is numb. Between explaining some version of what's going on to people, I've been working on a plan.

I've decided that if that school board meeting is happening tonight, I'm going to be there. Rebel says she and her group will be holding a rally outside. I asked her, "How would you feel about some musical accompaniment?"

Then I talked to several of my friends here—most agreed to join if they could get transportation. Our plan is to show that Atlantis is an excellent school—or could be. If we start treating it like it's part of the community, rather than something that's more important than the community.

At lunch, I risk being seen using my phone by the café monitors and shoot a quick update to Rebel.

"Are you going to speak at the school board meeting?" Fabiola asks. We slide into our usual seats. Taj is already there. So is Benz.

"Hey, guys," I say. I spear a cube of fresh pineapple onto my fork and pop it into my mouth. I love pineapple. I turn back to Fabiola and say, "My friend from MacArthur has been fighting to get better funding for my old school. I think Atlantis has to do more to recognize that it has a responsibility to reach out to the community it's in."

"MacArthur Park schools have always been sort of in the toilet," Taj says. I wince. "No offense." Hmm . . . too late. I'm offended.

"The district's not 'in the toilet.' It just doesn't get money and resources like other districts." I sound like Rebel now. But it's true.

Taj bites his sandwich, chewing loudly. "Well, no offense again, but I love having this new school that gives a chance at a proper, high-level music education *and* regular education. Are you saying, like some other people, that this school, Atlantis, shouldn't have ever been built? That the money should've gone into that . . . uh, into MacArthur Park schools?"

And that's the real question, isn't it?

The fight Rebel and I've been having from the beginning has been over whether or not the community needs a performing arts school.

Now, I know what I think. It is needed. A traditional school could never provide the specialized arts curriculum we're getting here.

But I have an idea about how we can share the resources.

"I'm not saying that at all. But wouldn't it be great if our school, Atlantis, as a community, offered outreach programs to kids in the community who can't get in or are too young? I think opening the school up to the community, offering after-school programming or special programming that brings in kids from MacArthur Park, would make the residents much less resentful of this place."

"I don't know," Taj says, chomping into his sandwich some more. "I hate to say it, but I've heard most of those kids from MacArthur Park are sort of ghetto. What if they come in here and tear our stuff up?"

No, he did not just say that! A twitch develops in my eye. I'm about to say something real tart when I get a sharp elbow in the ribs.

227

"Ow!" I rub my side.

"Look!" Fabiola shoves her phone under my nose. It's a video. Channel 7. Oh boy!

". . . in the home of Lotus Bloom and her mother, Willow Bloom. Ladies, good morning."

"Good morning, Sally," the video-me says to the interviewer.

"WSVN Channel 7 has learned that you've been given three days to either cut or change your natural hairstyle, or be expelled from the brand-new, multimillion-dollar school here in Miami Beach. Is that true?"

On the tiny phone screen, she is holding the letter that Penelope woman gave me yesterday. I nod at the letter.

"Yes, ma'am. That's the letter they gave me yesterday in my dean's office."

"So the Atlantis School administration is aware of this and is okay with it?"

"I'm . . . well, I guess. The way Mrs. Cortez made it sound, the board members were speaking on behalf of the school. So, yes, I guess so."

"And you were named concertmaster at the beginning of the school year based on your amazing talent, correct?"

"Yes."

"Would you mind playing for us?"

I played.

"Ms. Bloom, how do you and your . . . I mean, Lotus's father feel about the treatment of your daughter?"

"We think it's sad that bullies not employed by the school are using their power to intimidate children," Mom said.

The video switches back to a stand-up shot of Sally in the noonday news studio. She says:

"A number of neighborhood activists are gathering to protest the Atlantis School and what they think is the unfair allocation of public money for use on a school that is being treated like a private school. Now, with the inclusion of Miss Bloom, the Atlantis administration is being accused of mistreatment inside their school."

"Sounds like you're staying on top of a potentially volatile situation, Sally," says a man with sculpted Ken-doll hair. "I know our viewers will be waiting for your report after tonight's meeting. Now, Gray Skies is going to tell us all about the weather . . ."

The entire café is looking in my direction when I pass back Fabiola's phone.

I feel a runaway train racing through my veins. I'm teetering, practically shivering. Taj is still shoving food down his face, and his attitude, I don't mind saying, is disappointing. Benz, however, stands and moves behind my chair when he sees how shaky I am.

"Come on, Afro, you should go in the ladies' room. Throw some water on your face," he says.

Fabiola follows me, and I thank Benz before disappearing inside the restroom. I'm surprised and relieved to see Tati in there. She rushes over and puts her arms around me.

"Lotus! OMG! I came in here to change my contacts. Everyone is talking about your news segment. Why didn't you say anything this morning?"

I bark out a short laugh and fall against the sink.

"Honestly? I forgot about it. After they ambushed me and my mom . . ."

"You didn't call them?" Tati asks.

"Heck no!" I say. "Although, I'm sure my best friend did. But since their visit, I've been busy putting together a plan. I'm going to need some help. What are you guys doing tonight?"

I take five minutes telling them my plan.

"Count me in, for sure!" says Tati.

Fabiola agrees: "Whatever I can do."

☙

I thought I knew what to expect at the school board meeting.

No. I did not.

Mom and Granny decide they'll come to the school board meeting. Uncle Steve, too. I leave home early when Rebel and her parents swoop me up. I'd thought we were going to the interim school board headquarters.

"This is the staging area," Rebel says as we pile out of the car. We are in an open field. Or what would be an open field if it weren't for all the cars. It reminds me of being little back when Unk played for the U and we'd tailgate before his games.

"Are all these people here for the meeting?" I ask.

Police cars roam the edges of the field. Hammering sounds punctuate the evening air. Protest signs being attached to wooden pegs.

Soft air hangs around us, smelling of ocean and fresh-cooked popcorn. But beneath the festive air is a whiff of danger.

"It's like a festival!" I say, a bit disbelieving.

"Tonight is going to be big!" Rebel says. She breaks into a run across the field, and I realize she's heading right for Connor, who is standing with a wide Black man in a fancy suit.

Both her moms begin to chuckle.

"That's our baby," Janae says. She's taller than her wife and partner, Teal. I've always loved that name, Teal. She's small, like Rebel. She carried Rebel, who told me Teal had been inseminated with sperm from Janae's brother.

Rebel is a combo of both, with Teal's small features and Janae's light skin and hazel eyes.

Teal says, "That girl is never going to just settle, J. She gets that from you!" They chuckle again. I've always been a little envious of Rebel. When we were younger, I thought it was so awesome, having two mommies. When Mom and Dad were first splitting up, I wanted Mom to marry a lady so I could have two mommies, too.

Nowadays, my envy has to do with how unified her moms always are. How completely together they seem. Hard as I try, I can't ever remember a time when my parents seemed so perfectly in sync like that.

231

We catch up with Rebel and Connor in the middle of a huddle.

Rebel grabs ahold of the suit guy's arm and pulls him toward me. "Lotus, I want you to meet Rev. Hargrove. He's a community activist, and he's on our side!"

"Nice to make your acquaintance, young lady," he says. His manner is slick and practiced. I bet his church sermons are like theater. I instantly get bad vibes from him.

"Hello," I say. I look from Rebel to Connor to the moms. Teal jumps in.

"Lotus, honey, Rev. Hargrove here is taking up the cause of getting better funding for the schools," Teal says.

"That's right," the man's voice booms. My dislike grows. "And I hear they're threatening you, one of their best and brightest, because you refuse to bow down to their demands that you 'fit in' to some mold they're trying to put you in."

I feel like I've walked too close to the edge of a pool and accidently fallen into the deep end. This whole situation is drowning me. I fight the urge to give in to the drowning sensation.

This is the part where I'm supposed to be fearless and strong—pushed into action by my anger and knowing I'm right.

"I . . . I don't know what to say," is all I can muster, feeling shaken.

"Don't worry, Lo," Rebel says brightly. "We got you!"

"You got it ready, Reb?" Teal says to her.

"Yeah, Ma!" she says. Turning to me, she says, "Lotus! Come meet the rest of our team!"

Our team.

It turns out that there is a core group of volunteers who started out with Rebel. I meet the team, and she tells them who I am.

Before they can pepper me with questions, Rebel says, "No time for that right now. Now we have to make sure our signs are ready. The new meeting room will only hold about fifty of us. The cops will make sure of that. So everybody else needs to have signs and needs to be willing to show them."

Then she introduces me to a woman. "Jennifer Lopez," the woman says.

I blink. She's a pretty lady with long dark chestnut brown hair and large, round brown eyes. But . . .

"Not that Jennifer Lopez," she says in a way that tells me she's been saying that since before I was born. "I'm an attorney, and I'm running for the state representative seat in the 27th District. I want to assure you that I take your plight very seriously and if elected plan to do everything in my power to assure . . ."

My brain drifts off into musical scales. This lady is a walking, talking, glossy ad like the kind they run on TV when it's time to pick a new president.

When she finally finishes, I smile weakly. "Uh . . . um, nice to meet you," I say.

That's when I begin to notice that a number of the kids on the open field are wearing the same shirt Rebel has slipped on over her other shirt. I gasp when I read it:

#saveourschools

#savethewoollymammoth

She follows my gaze and grins. "Cool! Right?" When I don't respond, she goes on, "Here, put this on. I made one for you, too."

She passes the black T-shirt to me, and I drop it over my head, feeling numb. This whole situation is fast getting out of control.

Rebel picks up a megaphone. She is like a tiny general on her own battlefield. With the help of her moms, they work out more details.

"Are you excited?" Connor whispers to me once the general takes a pause.

"I . . . I think so," I say, suddenly feeling anchors wrap around my ankles.

"You'll be fine!" Rebel cuts in. "I'm so glad you joined us, Lotus. It's so great to have you back on our side."

There is something sinister about that. My mind starts to play the screeching violin sounds used to score the movie *Psycho*.

We talk through it—our plan. The sinister feeling grows. It's clear my friend has a set of things she wants to have happen. Our plan feels a lot more like her plan.

"Lo, you can bring these clowns to their knees. Tell

everybody how they've treated you. Tell them how the mae-stro elevated you and now you're being targeted out of jeal-ousy. And I have someone who is going to drop the word 'lawsuit.' That'll get their attention!"

My pulse thuds in my wrist, and heartbeats as low-down as bass drumbeats pound me from the inside out.

"Rebel, I didn't say anything about a lawsuit," I say, feel-ing my tongue go dry in my mouth.

She flicks her hand, as if my not wanting to start a lawsuit and her having someone threaten a lawsuit is just a minor point.

"You've got this, girl. You can change everything about how they recruit, which is a huge step toward showing that we need our schools improved—we don't need to recruit all the talent out of the neighborhood and turn our backs on everybody else."

I wish I had Rebel's confidence. She's so certain this will all work. I'm not. I'm not even certain what I want to have happen.

She wants to force the board to admit they will allocate millions of dollars to the MacArthur schools. Of course, I wish that, too.

But I can't help thinking she has something more up her sleeve. Like maybe the playbook she showed me isn't the only one she's using. What chance is there that the school board will magically renegotiate millions of dollars in funds based on a seventh grader?

Who knows? Maybe she has a better chance than I know.

For me, the goal is much simpler:

I want assurance that Monday, if I return to school with an afro, no one will try to usher me off the campus. Period.

And I want Adolpho and his mom to leave me alone.

My Atlantis posse arrives, and I introduce them to Rebel. They've brought their instruments, too.

Rebel says, "Showtime!" and we all start toward the entrance.

Space fills up quickly.

A man with thin hair and a heavy voice booms his baritone into the mic, making everyone wince. He calls the meeting to order.

"May I have everyone's attention, please," he booms. Cymbals clash and clang inside my body. I'm a walking symphony, only my internal instruments are all playing different tunes. Like fear, it's overwhelming and hard to turn off.

School board meetings must be what old-timers used to numb people with before surgery, back before anesthesia existed. I'm so bored! Between the monotone and the low-grade buzz of overhead fluorescent lights, not to mention the sea of neutral tones, I'm bored out of my mind.

But terror has a way of keeping your senses sharp.

And I am beginning to feel the grip of horror-movie terror. The kind of fear reserved for things that go bump in the night.

I look around the space, trying to spot my family, but I

don't see them. We're up front, like VIPs. The attorney lady and the reverend are with us.

We were made to leave all signs outside. Rebel was clearly anticipating that. Her group all has paper signs folded, hidden inside shirts, jackets, purse, whatever.

And one girl—it is hard to take my eyes off her—has written all over her face and skin—her bare arms, and legs, tops and bottoms of her limbs—all covered. Her skin is midnight dark, her 'fro is one-hundred-percent authentic, and her message is undeniable.

Peace.

Freedom.

Power.

Knowledge.

Love.

Over and over, the words are written in bright white paint. With her skin tone, she's almost glowing like a beacon.

"Cool, huh?" Rebel whispers when she catches me staring at the girl. "That's Monet Michelle. She goes to Freedom High. The moms are friends with her mom; that's how we met."

"She's hard to look away from," I say.

"That's the whole point!"

"Now, I open the floor up to the community. If there's anyone here wishing to speak before the board, please raise your hand. A school officer will come around with a microphone," says the loud man.

Right at that moment, I lock eyes with Dr. Cortez. She is standing almost out of sight. She is staring right at me, like she's daring me to say anything. Adolpho stands slumped next to her. When our eyes meet, he quickly looks away. Not his mom. I force myself to stare back.

"Go, go, go!" Rebel hisses, pushing me out of my seat. She actually pushes the underside of my elbow to make my arm go up. "Just like we planned."

It's like the world slows its motion. I push to my feet, knees wobbly. I'm glad the school officer let me bring in my violin case after looking inside. My stomach makes a disturbing noise, and I turn and look down at Rebel.

"Don't you dare get sick, Lotus Bloom! Do you hear me? Pull it together!" she hisses, wearing her scowl.

Like she's dealing with her dog, Maya, she speaks slowly to me in a calm voice:

"Don't you want to make them pay for how they've treated you? *Hmm*? Don't you want to tell your side of the story? Don't you want to wear your afro and not be judged?"

"Young lady," says a member of the school board, "would you please take the microphone and step into the aisle. State your name and your business with this board."

I am shaking all over.

Everyone is staring at me. Is it the perfectly pieced throwback outfit? Or the sky-high pineapple 'fro? I'm not sure.

The shaking inside me runs through my body to my

fingertips. The policeman guides me to the spot, and I move into it with the microphone.

Big inhale.

Rebel has helped me come up with what to say. Or am I about to simply say what she wants me to say?

Exhale.

"Hello," I say. Voice quavering, I clear my throat. "My name is Lotus Bloom."

21

I don't look at the lights in my eyes; don't listen to the doubts in my head.

"I'm a violinist. I'm here because . . . the county promised that the Atlantis School would welcome kids from all over the county. Kids who show the level of talent and commitment necessary to balance their artistic specialty with their regular academics."

I pause.

"I deserve the right to study at the Atlantis School. I deserve to be concertmaster. I earned that spot. I was chosen for the honor. I deserve to wear my hair"—I indicate my pineapple 'fro—"how I want without having paper airplanes dive bombing into me . . ."

"Stop it! Right this instant!" A shrill voice's demand crackles in the tightly packed room.

Heads turn. People crane to see, some standing to glance

over the sea of heads. Mrs., uh, um, Dr. Cortez is standing. Her body is pitched forward. Her usually practiced professional voice now high and reedy.

"I will not stand by and listen as this . . . this . . . person maligns our school!"

A board member smacks the tabletop with a judge's little hammer.

"Order! Order!" says the board member. "Dr. Cortez, you will have your moment if you so choose. Let the young woman continue."

The only Black person on the board holds up a hand. "Miss Lotus, are you the baby from the Channel 7 noon news program?"

"Yes, ma'am." When I look back at Rebel, she's giving me a thumbs-up sign.

"I am curious, Miss Lotus. Now, on the news, it said you were threatened with expulsion because they were throwing paper airplanes into your hair? Do I have that right?"

I am nodding, but once again I am cut off by Dr. Cortez.

"I demand that the board suspend this until further investigation! I respectfully request a closed-door session!"

That leads to an explosion.

"Hell no!" shouts another Black woman wearing one of Rebel's shirts. "That's how y'all rammed that Atlantis School down our throats. You had one of those 'closed-door' meetings, and when you came out, you'd taken all the money that should've stayed in our community and spent it on that school. Now you trying to run this little girl out. Over her afro? Chile, please!"

"Yeah!" come the shouts.

Yelling. Chanting.

"Order! Order!" yells the man bamming the little hammer against the table.

"This is the kind of mess y'all always pulling!" says a Black man in the middle of the room. His brown skin looks sweaty, and his eyes are outraged. "How you gonna say our kids have an equal chance when you kick the legs out from under us at every turn!"

More shouts.

"Yeah!"

"Right on!"

"You tell 'em!"

The policeman who'd led me to my spot in front of the microphone stand is now down front. He stands to the side of the raised seating where the board sits, hands in his belt loops. His eyes are scanning like he is waiting on a crime to occur.

I feel the microphone snatched from my hand. I'm not exactly surprised to see Rebel has joined me.

She says into the mic, "We can't have our schools improved? We can't improve our education by going to their new school. When is it our turn?"

The guy with the gavel hammers on the long table again

242

as a fresh round of chanting and shouting and wailing begins. Rebel's face is glowing. She is leading a deafening chant:

"No justice! No peace! No justice! No peace!"

I feel lost. And sick. My friends from Atlantis are no longer visible. Rebel's plan had been for me to stand up, declare war, and quit!

Yes, quit Atlantis.

Tell them I don't need their self-righteous, censorship-on-demand type of education. That last part was all Rebel.

Now?

Now I want a new plan. I want to say my piece, ask that I please not be expelled, then play a short piece of music for them with Tati and a few of our other friends.

However, the whole room is erupting into ugliness. Voices raised. Threats launched like grenades. My heart pounds its bassoon thrum in my ears.

Without even thinking about it too much, I thread my way down the aisle and up to the board's table. There is so much bedlam in the room, no one even seems to notice when I climb onto the table, sit in a cross-legged position, and open my violin bag.

I look out over the room, and what I see is a war. Not the bullet kind, but the social kind. People are shouting at one another, but no one is listening.

My most important tool, I tell myself, is my music. No matter what, music lives inside me, grows in my soul. No one can take that away.

No one is paying me any attention anymore. They're all shouting and yelling and screaming. I slink backstage for a minute, trying to catch my breath. My hands are shaking so bad, every time I try to lift my violin, it shakes in my hand.

I'm sitting in a cool cluster of shadows spilling from a wall of curtains. There's a performance space behind the meeting space. I remember that instead of their normal meeting spot, we're located in a community center.

I sit. Knees bent. Head down. I breathe in and out; in and out. Feelings and ideas jumble around.

A sound draws my attention. Nothing comes to mind at first. Then a rustle of fabric and the undercurrent of voices reach me. Someone is talking harshly.

I get closer.

Silhouettes. Shapes. Sharp hisses. A familiar scent.

I get closer.

Mrs. Cortez. And she's with Adolpho. Her thin lips stretch into a harsh line. Her voice is a snake's, dark and lethal.

". . . your fault. Losing your spot to a worthless little piece of trash like that."

Adolpho mashes the words in his throat. Fear?

". . . not my fault . . . you know I didn't want to be in orchestra this year anyway. I wanted to be in visual arts and join the anime club."

CRACK!

The sound is so shocking, I shrink back into the folds of

the curtains. She slapped him. Mrs. Cortez slapped her child. Then she slaps him again, this time with a hateful comment:

"You're as worthless as your father. Grow a backbone. I'm doing my best to give you culture and status. Stop looking for ways to undermine me!"

Her high heels strike the hard tile floors like railroad spikes being drummed on by children.

Truly shaken, I slip out of the shadows when I hear her pass and I go back to the front area. The arguing from the crowd continues. That's when I make my move. Up front, as central as possible. Shaking inside. But I calm myself. Slow the rhythm of my heart.

And I begin to play.

Marvin Gaye—"What's Going On."

At first, the soft strains in the beginning can barely be heard over the roar of protests. I lift my body until I'm standing on the table. I never stop playing. Eyes shut, I can't see the conflict—only the beauty.

The '70s antiwar anthem folds itself around me. I feel my body lean into the rhythm. The notes cry out. Desperate. Haunting. Lasting. In the lyrics, Marvin Gaye is making a plea to end war and stop fighting.

Those thoughts. The lyrics. The sentiment. They all move around me and lift me up. Is anyone in this room even listening? Can they hear me? I can't hear them.

I'm on my own journey. Eyes shut tight. I feel the message

of my music with my whole soul. I'm giving my whole soul to these people, and the effort leaves me weak.

Finally, the piece ends. Like always it takes a few seconds for me to come back. To be present.

This time, when I open my eyes, I am shocked to find everyone in the room is staring at me. The people at the table, the people in the audience, the unsure policeman.

My arm aches from the intensity of my bow work. My shoulders feel incredibly tight.

Every person in the space is staring open mouthed at me. Then applause, loud and forceful. My spirit is prancing like wild ponies. Wild ponies prance, right?

Shouts of, "More! More!" echo throughout the space. The little guy with the hammer continues to pound on the table, but no one can hear it. When the noise finally subsides, some man on the far side of the room stands.

One look at his sour face, and you can tell he's not a fan.

"It's all well and fine that the girl can play, but I don't want my son going to a school where kids don't know their place. Hair like that might be fine for other venues, but if it's causing problems at the school, I say why not do something with it!"

Now he gets applause. Several other people on his side of the room tack on to his comment with similar comments of their own.

The one Black woman at the table, the board member whose name plate reads Barbara Hawkins, says into a microphone,

"But you people are missing the point. From what I'm hearing, her hair isn't the problem. The problem is that there are students bullying her . . ."

Then she's drowned out.

"No one is 'bullying' her!" screeches that Cortez woman. And the argument sails around the space again.

And the anger returns.

My anger.

Feelings I've worked hard my whole life to push away. Never wanting to be angry or yell or have conflict. Never liking the way those feeling feel inside my body, like foreign objects.

Now it boils, and boils, and boils.

No one is listening.

Then I notice a figure moving from the shadows. Tall, straight shoulders, gliding up the carpeted aisle. It's Maestro.

"Maestro Vasquez, sir," blurts a member of the board, sounding nervous and looking sweaty and unsure.

"Sir!" says Maestro. His eyes are hard, but his movements are fluid, almost musical, like a dancer's.

He comes to stand directly in front of me, causing a rush of whispers and awed tones. I am still standing on the table. My violin and bow hang at my side.

"Miss Bloom," he says. I grit my teeth. Suddenly, I'm as angry at him as everybody else. He didn't want to see what was right in front of his face. He could've stopped this before it ever got this far. He was right there.

Instead of answering him, I hop down to the one microphone on a stand and screech out the *Psycho* theme on my violin. Loud and sharp and harsh notes reverberate through the speakers.

Several people cry out and press their hands against their ears.

"Miss Bloom, please," says Maestro. He reaches his hand toward me, but I push it away. Anger makes you bold!

Instead, I take the microphone and glare at all the faces across the room.

"Shame on all of you! Shame on the school for allowing one donor and 'steering committee' member to come in and bully them over how to run the school." I picture Adolpho backstage with his horrible mother and bite my tongue. I won't name him. I can't.

"And shame on the rest of you parents who showed up to support something you don't understand. Who came here to stand against one girl, me—for a hairstyle? We have kids at Atlantis who come to school with no hair on the sides of their heads and the tops painted in rainbow colors. And *I'm* the distraction?

"And shame on you!" I look over at the people at the table. "For completely dismissing schools in MacArthur Park like they're a lost cause. At the very least, Atlantis could work to share its resources with MacArthur. Offer tutoring in music and other arts. Allow the students to try out and participate in some of our programs. Why not? Why can't you come up with a way to bring the two schools together, the community, instead of pulling everything apart?"

"Miss Bloom, please," Maestro's voice is imploring. Only then do I realize tears are flowing down my cheeks.

"I hate this. I hate it here," I say, pulling away from Maestro, speaking in the microphone, voice crackling like my heart. "Don't worry about my afro. I'm leaving. If you're going to let someone like her"—I stab my finger at Mrs. Cortez—"dictate your policy, I'm done!"

Then I turn and rush blindly behind a veil of tears.

Out the side door, past the tiny garden, and down the block.

Away

   Away

      Away.

22

I am two blocks away before Uncle Steve catches up with me. Mom and Granny are in the car. They take me home, and I immediately lock myself in my room.

I am a mess.

Nothing has worked out the way I'd planned.

Me and Tati and a few others were supposed to play music and soothe everyone's frayed nerves. We were supposed to talk freely and openly. We were supposed to change hearts and minds.

I know that's not what Rebel had wanted, but it was . . . would have been the best solution.

Doesn't matter. Nothing matters now.

❧

The next morning I wake up and my whole body aches. Other than Mom's white ankle boots, I'm still fully clothed.

Which means I fell asleep with the woolly mammoth loose and free.

No good.

Then again—who cares!

There's a light knock at my door.

My instinct is to say, "GO AWAY!" But who has that kind of energy? I'm expecting Mom's face, but it's Granny. Her small eyes narrow into slits.

"Get up, gal, and shower. Then get on out here and have something to eat."

I glance at the clock by my bed. It's seven thirty. In the morning.

"Granny? What are you doing here?" I ask, sitting up.

"No time for all that now. Get your little butt up and shower. Change." She gives me a sly grin and says, "But don't change too much!"

She disappears into the hall.

What in the world did that mean?

My brain feels like oatmeal. And every part of my body feels sore. Like all the stress from my brain has wrung out my entire body. I slip inside the bathroom attached to my bedroom, grateful for the privacy.

The mirror this morning is not my friend. The scarf I'd worn to push up my 'fro into a pineapple is now half around my neck. My hair is sticking out and up and everywhere. And the bags under my eyes are more like luggage. A full set.

I stay in the shower for hours. For days. For years.

Steam and hot water. Buttery soapsuds and lather.

The shower is raindrops playing a xylophone's tinkling music as it plinks against the porcelain tub.

By the time I get out, my skin has reddened and my hair is good and damp. I slather leave-in conditioner in it, pull on my robe, and head back to my room.

I pull on a pair of loose, comfortable shorts and an old T-shirt from my days at music camp a few years back. It's still too big, which does give me a giggle.

Voices filter through the floorboards. Old Florida pine boards. A man's voice? Uncle Stevie's here, no doubt. I heave a huge sigh. Might as well go and get this over with. Already I can feel another rotten day coming on.

I'm not prepared for the scene that's waiting for me.

Mom. Granny. Uncle Steve. Not surprising. However, the tall man in the suit, the woman, and . . .

"Dad!"

"Baby!" he says. I'm running to him before he can even finish the word. He wraps his arms around me, and I bury my head in his shoulder.

"I didn't know you were coming! Why are you here? What are you doing?" I start to babble.

He laughs. "Glad to see you, too, ma chère," he says with a chuckle. "We can get into all that later. For now, you have guests."

I turn and face the two strangers. The man, tall—very

tall—turns. He's holding one of Mom's special china cups. The ones she never uses. Oh, so we fancy now?

"Lotus!" He says my name like we know each other, even though we don't. "I'm Superintendent Charlton Burr, and this"—he turns to the woman—"is district coordinator and attorney Ms. Jessica Aguirre. It is good to meet you."

"Nice to make your acquaintance," the woman says, and I see she also has a cup of Mom's wedding china.

"Good morning," I say, feeling extremely underdressed. The woolly mammoth is drenched in conditioner, and I'm meeting strangers in my don't-leave-the-house clothes.

"Let's everybody sit until . . . ," the superintendent begins, but he's interrupted by the doorbell. I'm clinging to Dad's finger, my pinkie grasping his, the way me and Tati had done before the school board meeting where everything turned upside down.

"Ah," says the tall man, "he's here."

I look at Mom, and she looks at me with a smile I can't quite read. The door opens, and I hear a familiar voice join our strange assembly.

"Miss Bloom, good morning!" says Maestro.

After a few more minutes of offering coffee and getting settled in our living room, Superintendent Burr begins:

"First, let me say to you folks that I'm so sorry for the way Lotus has been treated. None of this should have happened. Dr. Cortez and her contingent have been valuable fundraisers and did indeed work tirelessly to assure the school fundraising project was a success.

"However, they had no authority—none—to dictate policy or in any way skew opinions of who should be attending our school and how. Miss Bloom, Lotus, the idea that your natural hair isn't acceptable in our school is absurd. My own daughter wears an afro at Miami Day School. It's unbelievable that this matter has gotten so out of hand!"

Either he is a master actor or his reaction is real. He appears aggravated, frustrated, and confused.

"Well, thank you for that," Dad jumps in, "truly. But why didn't you put an end to it immediately?"

"I assure you, as soon as I was aware of it, I did. I've been on an extended educational training along with the dean of the Atlantis School. Dean Mackie, normally the assistant in charge of seventh grade, has been overwhelmed and was clearly no match for the formidable Ms., uh, Dr. Cortez. I assure you, I will remedy the situation."

The grown-ups chirp at one another about policies and this and that. My head swims. Someone clears his throat. It's Maestro.

"Miss Bloom, what I don't understand is why you didn't bring this to my attention immediately. I could have ended it at once," he says.

My eyes bug.

"I did. Well, I . . ." My voice falters. "I sort of did. I mean, you gave me that speech about managing people and being in charge. You made it sound like . . . like if I were older, I'd be able to take care of any problem."

I swallow hard, hearing the exhaustion in my voice. Feeling the weight of the past several weeks in my bones. I fight the urge to climb onto the couch, tuck my knees into my chest, and rest my face on my dad's thigh.

Maestro taps the side of his cup with one long finger.

"I apologize, Miss Bloom. Lotus." It's the first time I've ever heard him say my first name. He pronounces it using two distinct syllables—Lo-*tus*. "I must admit, when I am involved in music, in helping the students understand the music, I get lost. I don't see everything that I should. If someone needs help and I don't see, I count on my concertmaster to do it. I never considered that my concertmaster would be the one in need."

Mom moves to sit at the other end of the sofa.

Granny, standing with her arms crossed, grunts.

"Well, no offense to none of ya, but that still don't fix the two big issues far as I see," she says with a sniff. "For one thing, my baby here earned her spot in your fancy school, got threatened because of her hair, and now she done gone and quit. What we gonna do about that? And another thing, the bigger thing, whether she stay there or come back to her old school, what's gonna be done to help these children at her old school?"

All right, Granny!

I look at her, and she looks back. For the first time this

morning, I feel myself grin and sit up straighter. I find my voice, too.

"Granny is right. I meant what I said last night. I've been volunteering at the rec center where Unk—uh—Uncle Steve is in charge. The little dudes are great. I love them, and they love learning. But when I look at the shabby instruments, versus the resources we have at Atlantis, it makes me want to cry," I say.

Granny gives me at little smile, and I smile back.

Mr. Burr looks at the attorney lady and gives her a slight nod. She nods back, and he turns to the rest of us.

"Believe it or not, we've already been looking at ways to—as you said last night—share the resources. I am putting together a committee of parents, teachers, and students from both schools to look for ways we can work together. Would you be willing to participate? We could use someone with your insight, Miss Bloom."

I look from Mom to Dad.

"Yeah, sure. I'd love to," I say.

"And finally," Maestro begins, turning so that his warm brown gaze is focused a hundred percent on me, "you, my concertmaster. You simply cannot leave. I was being honest when I said you are one of the most gifted, unique young violinists I've ever had the pleasure of meeting. You must allow me to continue to challenge you, guide you, and shape you. You must let me contribute to your development. I want to be able to say I knew her when . . ."

He graces me with a rare ear-to-ear smile.

I smile back.

"Mom? What do you think?"

She seems surprised. I'm asking her and not Dad. But I want her input. She smiles, too.

"I want to see you stand up and fight! If being there is what you want. Go get it!"

Well, all right, Mom!

I reach out my hand to Maestro, and he takes it. "It's a deal," I say.

"Oh," Mr. Burr says, grinning as well, "I don't suppose you've seen the *Herald*?"

I shake my head, and the attorney lady reaches for a folded newspaper tucked under her arm and passes it to me.

The paper crinkles as it unfolds. I let out a squeak, gasp, and drop the paper on the floor. Everyone laughs, including Mom and Granny. I drop to my knees, grab the paper, and make a closer inspection.

A huge headline topping the front page of the B section reads:

AFRO REVOLUTION
School Board Special Session Erupts;
Music Student Fights Expulsion Over
Natural Hair!

Beneath the photo is a picture of me. Standing on the table. School board members looking up at me. Violin thrust beneath my chin. Afro in midsway.

"Oh. My. God!" I say, sitting back on my feet in disbelief.

Granny grins. "You dang right!"

In the brief moment of silence that follows, I hear the notifications chime on my phone, *ding, ding, ding.* I race to the bedroom, grab my cell off the nightstand, and return to where the grown-ups are waiting.

"Lean in, everybody!" I say.

They laugh, but do as I ask.

"Say, 'Woolly!'"

I snap the photo and immediately post #woollymammoth #woollywins.

❦

"So when were you going to tell us about this whole moving-to-Paris scheme you'd cooked up?" Dad says later that day.

We're at lunch. Just the three of us.

The school board people and Maestro are off to do their thing after making me promise not to give up. Now, the three of us are sitting in an outdoor café beneath green awnings, facing the ocean and catching snatches of Latin music as cars cruise past. It's a beautiful day. Really beautiful.

"It . . . well, it's what I thought I wanted. I thought moving to Paris, especially after all the trouble started, would be the perfect solution. I just missed you so much, Dad. And the idea of you living this great life as a musician—in Paris—I wanted that, too," I say.

Mom looks wounded, and I hate myself a little.

"I got that letter," Mom says, her voice small, "the one about you applying for a scholarship to the fancy school, and I didn't know what to do about it. I've only had it a few days," she assures me.

"Lotus, you can't shut me and your mom out of your life like that," Dad says. He sips his bottled mineral water. "Look, maybe moving in with me *would* be the best thing for you . . ."

"NO!" Mom explodes.

Dad's face clouds, and I see shades of the school board meeting all over again.

"Stop!" I say, half rising from my seat. "Stop it! I'm not moving anyway. No offense, Dad, but Mom is right. Running off to Paris isn't what I need. I have a life here. Friends here. Opportunity here." I pause, then reach for her hands. "And a mom here. This is home."

Slowly, the clouds in his face clear. He knows I'm right.

"And your music, everything we've worked for?"

"My music will be fine," I say. "I'll be fine. Not to mention, I will be coming to Paris in December. That is, if I can come up with the six-hundred-dollar travel fee . . ." The two of them exchange glances, but to my surprise they say in unison:

"I can manage that."

For the next hour, we talk. Really talk. And I'm as honest as I know how to be. We're all learning still.

The conversation with Rebel later isn't quite so successful.

"So you're going to let them buy you back with promises of 'doing better'? Is that it?" she says, putting air quotes around "doing better."

"Rebel, quitting is just giving Mrs. Cortez and her cronies exactly what they want. They deserve to have me there, reminding them that kids like me, from where we come from, are just as good as they are. And I deserve to be there. You of all people should see that!"

We're in a tiny playground near my spot of zen on the beach, sitting on the swings. My toe digs into the sand and the cat-eyed shades on my face glint in the sunlight. Sunlight floods every surface, except Rebel's face, which is hopelessly cloudy.

"This is so typical of you, Lotus! Everything last night went perfectly! You were amazing! You stood up to those goons! Held your ground and made yourself heard. Now they're listening. Go back now and they've won. They've won, and MacArthur Park schools, this school, is toast."

"That's not true, Rebel. I really believe if . . ."

"Awww, forget it!" she says, launching herself off the swing.

I watch her stalk away.

In the distance, gulls cry and screech. Traffic lurches in fits and stops. I hold on to the chain links of the swing, rocking back and forth in the seat.

"She's got a temper," a voice says.

260

"Tati! What are you doing here?"

She shrugs.

"I was worried about you. I came by your house, and your mom told me I might find you here."

"I don't think she's going to forgive me," I say dejectedly.

"Maybe she will. If you're right, that is." She drops onto the swing that Rebel vacated. For several seconds we swing side by side in silence. Nothing can prepare me for the next voice I hear:

"Hey," he says.

"Adolpho!" both Tati and I say in surprised unison.

He's looking at the ground, hands in his pockets.

"Hey," I say. I stick my toe out, catching the sand to stop my motion. "What are you doing here?"

"Came to apologize," he says, still looking down. Finally, he turns to face us both. Says, "I wanted you to know, this whole thing got so blown out of proportion. My mom . . . she just doesn't know when to quit. I'm . . . I'm really sorry," he says, finally making eye contact.

I stare at him for a moment. He really means it. I'm sure.

"She's really mad," he goes on. "But me and my dad told her she went too far and she better fix it. I'm not sure what she can do, but when she sets her mind to it, she can make things happen. I think if you and those committee people tell her what the MacArthur kids need, she'll get it done. She has to. One thing my mom hates more than anything is failing!"

We laugh at that. He's probably right.

"What now?" I ask.

He shrugs.

"What else? Practice. We have a holiday concert to get ready for in a few weeks. And"—he pauses—"you have to get ready to perform in Paris."

Ahhh, yes!

Paris.

I'm looking forward to going and performing with the International Youth Orchestra.

And then I'm looking forward to coming home!

ACKNOWLEDGMENTS

I would like to acknowledge all of my family and friends who tolerate me and my ceaseless need for validation during my writing process. That includes my sisters—Jennifer and Janice—as well as my studious daughter, Kenya, and my hilarious nephew, Daelyn.

I'd like to pay special acknowledgment to middle school orchestra teacher Joanna Sell, who was willing to sit down with me and explain what the environment was like inside the world of young musicians. Thank you, Joanna, and thank you to my agent, Laurie Liss of Sterling Lord Literistic, for believing in what I have to say.